MRS ELTON
in
AMERICA
and other stories inspired

by characters created by

Jane Austen

and herewith comprising

The Compleat Mrs Elton

from the pen of

DIANA BIRCHALL

EGERTON HOUSE PUBLISHING

Published 2004 by Egerton House Publishing
Egerton House
3 Egerton Road
Bexhill on Sea
East Sussex TN39 3HH
United Kingdom

MRS ELTON IN AMERICA
and other stories
inspired by characters created by *Jane Austen*
and herewith comprising
The Compleat Mrs Elton

This edition first published 2004
ISBN NUMBER: 1-905016-018

Publisher's Note

Diana Birchall, who successfully took Mrs. Elton's side in her *In Defense of Mrs. Elton,* here reprinted, tells more of her story: *The Courtship of Mrs. Elton* and the adventurous *Mrs. Elton in America* finish *The Compleat Mrs. Elton* trilogy.

The History of Mrs. Elton

The first of these stories about Mrs. Elton, the outrageously ill mannered and vulgar character from Jane Austen's *Emma*, was conceived in a new and unusual fashion: *In Defense of Mrs. Elton* first appeared as an online serial for the two Jane Austen literary lists, Austen-l and Janeites. List members were discussing the lady's character, and I volunteered to defend her, doing so in episodes of a story that ran for many successive weeks. In trying to dredge up anything positive to say about Mrs. Elton, I discovered to my surprise that there was actually a good deal. It had always seemed to me that when she first arrived in Highbury, as a newcomer, a bride, unsure of her social position, she wanted to be friendly and to be accepted, and so she did things like propose to Emma that they unite to form a musical society. Yet the better-mannered characters always reacted as if she were odious and her suggestions appalling. While relating the events in *Emma* as seen from Mrs. Elton's viewpoint, I noticed that if you cut away Jane Austen's editorial perspective, Mrs. Elton's behaviour was open to a more sympathetic interpretation: Austen cunningly presented her in an unsympathetic way, while treating Emma herself quite tenderly, though Emma's own behaviour was not, in reality, any better than Mrs. Elton's.

Such discoveries made *In Defense of Mrs. Elton* an effective argument, and the story became something of a popular success, in its own peculiar genre. It was published by the Jane Austen Society of North America (JASNA) as its conference gift for 1999, and also had English and Australian editions. So I pursued my heroine in two more Mrs. Elton stories, *The Courtship of Mrs. Elton*, which tells of her life before she married Mr. Elton and came to Highbury, and the longer *Mrs. Elton in America*, which might be described as an historical comedy.

I had always considered that Mrs. Elton had some sort of mystical relation to America. As I mentioned in the preface to *In Defense of Mrs. Elton*, it may have been the fact of my growing up in New York that made me personally identify with the lady: her brassy, aggressive behaviour was the way New Yorkers are taught to behave so they won't get trampled. Mrs. Elton was a crassly behaved outsider, the Other if you like, as self-conscious visiting Americans sometimes feel they are in certain segments of English society. That's why I felt inspired to come to Mrs. Elton's defense, after she had been laughed at and abused for nearly two hundred years by the reading public, all because her creator, Jane Austen, was "partial and prejudiced" in her portrayal of the character.

It was only a step from these partisan thoughts and feelings to take Mrs. Elton, in actuality, to America itself, and see how she fared. She had a real life model: in 1827, Frances Trollope, mother of the not yet famous novelist Anthony Trollope, journeyed to the United States and wrote acerbic observations that were published as *The Domestic Manners of the Americans*. This book was a sensation in England, and did much, along with writings by Dickens and others, to form British social attitudes about Americans. I have always loved "fish out of water" stories that contrast the cultures of England and the United States; another of my favorite authors, Frances Hodgson Burnett, often treated such themes, in children's books (*Little Lord Fauntleroy*) and adult novels, such as *A Fair Barbarian*, which might be described as

Lily Bart goes to Cranford. So I set out to construct an English/American story of contrasts, with these models.

The events of Emma are supposed to take place in 1815; Mrs. Elton, setting out with her family on a missionary journey some ten years after her marriage, would have been contemporaneous with Frances Trollope, and her experiences in some ways parallel hers. Mrs. Elton observes, contends with, and has something to say about society in Boston and New York, slavery in the South, wild Indians in the West, as well as Canadian society. How her wide-ranging tour affected her character, the reader is about to discover.

So that the entire Mrs. Elton *oeuvre* can be entirely consumed in one gulp, the decision was made to publish all three Mrs. Elton stories in a *Compleat Mrs. Elton* volume. I trust this does not seem like too much of the lady, for I believe she will live in my heart forever. And speaking of hearts, I will only beg that purist readers who complain that the sending of Valentine Cards had not yet been invented in 1815, should please accept this anachronism, which was devised only for the sake of enabling me to have the pleasure of writing an acrostic on the immortal name of AUGUSTA HAWKINS.

Diana Birchall

The Compleat Mrs Elton

Contents

The Courtship of Mrs Elton

Augusta arrives in Bath

rank Churchill first saw Miss Woodhouse in February; and February was also the month which witnessed the meeting of Mr. Elton and Augusta Hawkins in Bath. There was little hope of finding much society in Bath at such a season, but even in the short and gloomy days of February, Augusta figured to herself that she would be more in company, and seen by more persons of elegance, than could happen at her uncle's lodgings in Birmingham, or in the retirement of Maple Grove. If a young woman does not find a husband at home, she must venture farther afield; and fortunate it was for Augusta, that in her eight or nine years of young ladyhood, she had contrived a network of friends and acquaintances who were all alive with eagerness to welcome her as the most desirable guest there could possibly be. Any fee for such service as they provided was trifling, hardly worth mentioning; and Augusta would have paid much more than the sum she gave to Mrs. Partridge, for the privilege of making her home in Bath during the tedious winter weeks that must intervene until she might have hopes of the spring campaign.

Mrs. Partridge was upon the watch, and as soon as Augusta was fairly seated in her front parlour, and the man-servant had conveyed her trunk upstairs to the best bedroom, her hostess was ready to recite her catalogue of personages in Bath who might be worth the attentions of a Miss Hawkins. Mrs. Partridge was a plump, bustling body, whose widowed state did not prevent her from being fond of gossip. If she was reduced to making shift to live by the expedient of taking in a boarder or so, they were never given that name, and were always of the very best sort; and now that she had married off her daughter, Miss Clara, to a fine gentleman who served in an attorney's office, and was known to Miss Hawkins' uncle, she had no more pressing business than to find a husband for Miss Hawkins herself.

This triumphant daughter, Mrs. Jeffereys, was also arrived to welcome Miss Hawkins, together with her two bosom friends, the Miss Milmans, the younger of whom was in that happy and superior state of being engaged before her elder sister. The whole party greeted their visitor with cries of delight, and urged that she would refresh herself by drinking a dish of tea; but it was hardly brought, before the important subject of matrimonial affairs had already been fairly thoroughly canvassed.

Miss Hawkins began with proper congratulations to Mrs. Jeffereys upon her marriage.

"Oh! my dear Augusta, you cannot conceive the happiness of being a married woman, at least, of being married to such a fine man as my Mr. J. Do you know, he never takes spirituous liquor - and he has the dearest little feet in the world, perfect marvels for elegance - and he absolutely adores me, I cannot tell you how much."

"That is all as it should be, my dear Mrs. Jeffereys; I am extremely glad. And Miss Susan - I hear that my congratulations are to be called for again, as you, too, are to enter Hymen's lists."

Miss Susan, a pretty but excessively silly girl, made her best simper. "You are too kind, Miss Hawkins. Yes, only think, I am to be married before Philly here - I never expected such a thing, upon my word, as I am only seventeen, and *she* is four and twenty; but Mr. Cooper would not have it otherwise, however much I positively made a nuisance of myself, with pleadings and urgings. Mr. Cooper, I said, you do me too much honour; are you absolutely sure you do not prefer my sister Philly? She is seven years older than me, so has much better sense, you know, even though the gentlemen do think me prettier. I should never dream of being insulted if it should turn out that he really loved her instead of me, but he would not hear a word of it. So Belle is to be an old maid after all. After five and twenty, there can be no hope of being married; but I tell her she will always have a home with me and my dearest Mr. Cooper, who is all benevolence."

Augusta, who was five and twenty herself, was not so cheered by this speech as to offer Miss Susan the satisfaction of any farther rejoicings, but Mrs. Partridge reassured both young ladies.

"Five and twenty! For shame, Miss Susan, that is not in the grave yet. There have been ever so many cases of ladies being married older than that. And I am determined, Miss Hawkins and Miss Milman, howsoever old you be, that you shall be off my hands before you are a month older - that I am; and you know yourself, my dear Clara, that even though it is dead of winter, Bath is filled with single young gentlemen of rank and fortune, more than ever was seen before."

"You are right, mama," said Mrs. Jeffereys complacently, "I know my dear Mr. J. has such hosts of friends, and I shall be very glad to introduce Miss Hawkins and Miss Milman to them all. That is - I do not know if I dare venture to make them known to Sir Cecil Crowthers, that might be looking a little too high, a baronet, after all, wants only to know baronet's blood, though he makes an exception in his friendship with Mr. Jeffereys - but there are some very fine men amongst his friends, all here playing cards and having ever such a nice time."

"I know who you are thinking of, Clara," said Miss Susan, winking hard, "I do indeed; and it will never do. Mr. Bird is a very fine fellow, and wears the very handsomest light-coloured breeches and figured waistcoat in all of Bath, but he is too young. He is not two and twenty. He will not suit my sister or Miss Hawkins. There are some older men - widowers and the like - military men retired on half-pay - that will be much more the thing for them."

"Dear me, how you talk, Miss Susan," cried Mrs. Partridge with energy. "Mr. Bird is only two or three - or four or five - years younger than the young ladies, and he has a good fortune. That is, I do not suppose he has any money of his own, but his older brother is a very well-off gentleman, with a fine house in Kent, and makes Mr. Bird a very handsome allowance. Sure, he is quite worth your attention, Miss Augusta; and you will see him, too, this very evening at the Rooms, for I know he told Miss Milman he would be there tonight, as will all the town, to be sure."

"Oh! I don't know what he told me," said Miss Milman, tossing her head, "he is such a puppy, I declare I could not listen to one word in three that he said."

"Well, well, you are nice in your taste, but I will tell you what, Miss Milman, you will not get a husband if you go on at that rate, being so severe upon the men. I daresay Mr. Bird is no Solomon - but he is single, and has no wife hid away anywhere about him, so you should make up your mind to take him if he asks you."

"I saw a most handsome clergyman walking about the town, this noon," contributed Mrs. Jeffereys, good-naturedly. "Excessively handsome. They do say he is just come, and has a good house and fortune, and is looking for a wife. I will tell you what, Miss Hawkins, if you are not too tired from your journey, we can step out this minute and look at the shops, and I will see if I can catch sight of this gentleman for you. I am sure to be able to contrive a meeting. I must go to the shops in any case, as I cannot endure the trimming upon my hat a moment longer, and have vowed that I shall never tire my dearest Mr. J. by appearing in the same hat trimming twice. Will you walk out with me, my dear Miss Hawkins? I am sure we will see something of this handsome clergyman. Mr. Elton is his name."

The Compleat Mrs Elton

The First Hour of Introduction

*M*rs. Jeffereys, the two Milmans, and Miss Hawkins went walking; and their search was rewarded almost before it began, for standing in plain sight, before the most important draper's shop in the Town, were two gentlemen whom Mrs. Jeffereys' eyes, sharpened as they were with a true matchmaker's penetration, descried at once as Mr. Bird and the very selfsame clergyman she had hoped to discover. The two gentlemen bowed, the ladies curtseyed, and introductions were swiftly made.

Mr. Bird, a friend of Mrs. Jeffereys' husband, was a tall young man with a very youthful face, and an expression of contented silliness; but his companion, equally tall, was both handsome and genial, and of very prepossessing manners. What the gentlemen were, must wait to be discovered, but Augusta's business at the moment was to make herself pleasing to both of them. The conversation, as it must be in the first moments, was mere formalities; but Mr. Bird rapidly unbent, and after some polite inquiries after the health of Mr. Jeffereys, he embarked upon an explanation of how he had met Mr. Elton.

"I have been at the draper's to order a new cravat; a very fine cravat, something quite new, for the Rooms: blue, I thought, a robin's egg blue, would be quite the 'ton'; and what was my surprise, Mrs. Jeffereys, but to meet an old friend, quite an old friend, in Philip Elton?"

"It is delightful when old friends meet again," said Miss Susan, with something between a laugh and a gurgle.

"You had known one another previously?" asked Augusta pleasantly, her eyes fixed upon Mr. Elton's face.

"Exactly so, Miss Hawkins. In fact, we were at school together, and poor Bird was my fag. I fear I was not very merciful to him."

"Come now, Mr. Elton, you cannot dissemble with *me*. I am perfectly sure you would show mercy to anyone in an inferior position," said Augusta.

"Why, I should hope so, now that I am in orders; but as a boy you know, boys are not very noted for that sort of thing."

"La! how shocking, Mr. Elton. Do tell us, Mr. Bird, what sort of a boy your friend was, I am longing to know," Miss Susan begged.

"Oh, Philip was always good-natured - certainly," said Mr. Bird. "The only thing wrong with him was that he did not care enough for his costume: but if he was a bit of a sloven, he is very much improved now."

The ladies laughed deprecatingly. "That is not much of a compliment, Bird. But I should expect no better of you - you who were always a fop, and to this day care a good deal more for your fine linen and your cravats than for riding or hunting."

"That is an accusation, indeed," said Augusta. "Do you hunt, Mr. Elton?"

He brightened. "To be sure I do, but I seldom get the opportunity, in these days. My parish duties you know..."
The conversation continued, no one saying anything more than ordinarily witty or clever; but in the minds of Mrs. Jeffereys and the Milman sisters, the impression was forming that Mr. Elton was very much attracted by Miss Hawkins, and that their intercourse might very nearly deserve to be given the name of flirting.

Mr. Bird was of this opinion too, and was not best pleased by it, as he thought Miss Hawkins handsome, and she had been represented to him as an heiress of useful, if not large, fortune. He was also so vain, as not to like any young lady being attracted to any gentleman but himself, and he was not inclined to allow all the attentions to Miss Hawkins to be on Mr. Elton's side. Accordingly, as the ladies began to think of suggesting that they take leave - since they really could not spent the whole afternoon standing talking in the street - Mr. Bird said, as if newly struck by the idea: "I say, Mrs. Jeffereys, have you been bid to the dinner at the Greens'? I know you are acquainted with them, and seldom miss."

"Why, yes, Mr. Bird, Mr. Jeffereys and I will be there, and my mother - all of our party, in fact."

"That is exactly what I hoped to hear. Green is such an hospitable host - every thing in the best style. No pitiful doings. I was sure you would be there."

"Shall I have the pleasure of seeing you at Mr. Green's dinner, Miss Hawkins?" Mr. Elton asked, with a particularity that was lost by no one present except possibly Miss Susan, who was ogling a woman in a really handsome hat who happened to be passing.

"Why yes - I believe - that is, I do not care much for going into company where there are many people I do not know - I am very retiring, in my way, if you can believe such a thing of poor me; but Mrs. Partridge was most urgent that I be of the party, and it does seem that I may find friends there."

"Friends! Exactly so," exclaimed Mr. Elton, gazing down at Miss Hawkins complacently, while Mrs. Jeffereys and Miss Milman exchanged significant looks.

The Compleat Mrs Elton

The Accidental Recontre

*T*he ladies took in all the sights and card parties of Bath, as everybody did, in and out of the season. There was nothing new in this social round to Augusta, with her eight seasons' experience of the place; but it did often occur to her, in the course of her multifarious activities, that, of all the people she had met during them, none had ever been more attractive to her than this Mr. Elton. He was very handsome, and decidedly agreeable; that he liked her was beyond question; and the Miss Milmans had swiftly found out, and swiftly related to her, that he was installed in an excellent and modern vicarage in one of the very finest towns of England, as well as being possessed of a comfortable competence of his own. Augusta had lived enough years in the world to know that she could hardly do better; that this might, indeed, be her last and best chance; and though she did not call herself desperate, she had already made up her mind, before she set eyes upon him for the second time, that, if he were ever to ask her to marry him, she would accept. Before this could transpire, it would be necessary for her to see him again, however; and accordingly she scanned every grouping of people with great attention, but she was unlucky. Mr. Elton was not to be seen, and she could only reassure herself with the thought that their next meeting would be at the house of Mr. Green.

Mr. Green was a very rich man, known to Mrs. Partridge, as was everyone worth knowing in Bath, because he had no aristocratic pretensions to debar him from her society: he had made his fortune in trade, and his wife had been a miller's daughter. There was no *cachet* in being a guest in their home, but Augusta had three distinct pieces of consolation: she would undoubtedly be the first lady in company; there would be a very fine dinner laid; and she would see Mr. Elton.

It was absolutely essential that all portions of her outfit for the important occasion should be perfect; and Augusta spent many a morning with Mrs. Partridge and her female intimates, discussing the gown, the mantle, the feathers, and the finery. On the very morning of the dinner, what was her concern to discover, in a preliminary examination of her stores, that she had not one pair of silk stockings that was without a ladder, a splash of mud, or some other imperfection. It was a small errand, such a very small one that she did not trouble to summon her confederates, or even the maid, who was hurrying to finish some sewing that would complete Augusta's costume. There was a shop where stockings could be procured, only a five minutes' walk away, and surely no elaborate preparations need be undertaken. On a drizzly morning, she was unlikely to meet with anyone she knew, in the course of such an errand, least of all Mr. Elton; and so she pulled on her common cloak and paid no special attention to her hair-dressing.

But Augusta's calculations were at fault, for as she hurried out of Drew's, a humble little parcel of stockings in her hand, she walked almost full up against that selfsame Mr. Elton. He caught her with his hand, prevented her parcel from falling, and could almost not apologize enough for the mishap.

"My dear Miss Hawkins! is it you! I am so extremely sorry. Have I hurt you with my clumsiness? Do pray tell me that I have not. I would not have injured you for the world."

Augusta assured him that she was intact, and somewhat flustered, she attempted to slip her parcel into her reticule, lest he discover what it contained.

"Oh! I have harmed your goods. Only assure me that your purchase is undamaged - allow me to restore it - shall we go into this shop and buy some more? Do permit me. Was it the glovers'? The silk merchant's?"

Augusta most sincerely begged that he would not trouble himself in the least, and gripped her reticule more firmly. "Do you - do you often come this way?" she ventured.

"No - that is, to say the truth, I have been laid up in my lodgings all this week with a slight cold, which I would not pass on to my friends for anything; but I am quite recovered again, and was actually on my way to pay a call upon you."

"Upon me!"

"Yes, Miss Hawkins, you. You cannot but be aware that you made a powerful impression on me at our meeting the other day; and in short - in short - "

Augusta summoned up the most encouraging look she knew how to bestow, but Mr. Elton did not seem to know how to proceed.

"Are you going home now? May I accompany you?" he asked helplessly.

She smiled. "Yes, certainly. It is early yet; perhaps you would care to have a dish of tea with us, before it is time to prepare for the dinner at Mr. Green's."

"The dinner at Mr. Green's! Oh, yes, by all means - I had forgot - I am to see you there tonight. Well, upon my word, that is so very..."

"Yes. I am looking forward to it I confess."

"And so am I. Exactly so. Well, Miss Hawkins, then, a lady ought not to walk home alone in all this wet; you might slip. Allow me to take your arm."

Miss Hawkins allowed it.

The Compleat Mrs Elton

The Dinner at Mr Green's

*T*he party that assembled in the Greens' drawing room was elegant in its appearance, though less so in mind, for the society there collected was not notable for anything more than dull repartee and commonplace remarks.

Mr. Jeffereys had bought a new gun, and wanted to tell every one who would listen about its features, as it was the very latest of its kind; but his usual confidante, Mr. Bird, had determinedly affixed himself to the side of Miss Hawkins, and would not attend. Augusta had Mr. Elton on her other side, and wanted very much to continue her conversation of the morning with him; but was prevented by Mr. Bird whispering in her ear. She tried to discourage him, for every time he spoke, Mr. Elton glowered; but she had little success. Mr. Bird had hold of a fold of material of her gown, and he pulled it urgently as he went on:

"Miss Hawkins - my dear Miss Hawkins - you must listen. I tell you I have written something for you. A very particular production. It is, in fact - a poem!"

"You don't say, Mr. Bird? - " turning to Mr. Elton. "I am sorry. What were you saying to me of Highbury?"

"Highbury is a very musical society, Miss Hawkins. I am sure you would like it. I know you would. Why, Miss Woodhouse has had the best masters from London to teach her to sing and to play; Mrs. Weston is a most accomplished musician; and Mrs. Cole has been saying that she means to purchase a new pianoforte for her daughters. Could you but visit in Highbury, I know you would be delighted."

"I am sure I should. Is your vicarage quite within the town itself, then, Mr. Elton?"

Mr. Bird pulled her skirt again. "Do let me read it to you, Miss Hawkins. Only once, must you hear it from my lips; and then I shall make you a fair copy to keep. Only listen - "

She was forced to turn away from Mr. Elton, and listened in vexation, annoyed with herself for blushing angrily, as Mr. Bird read what appeared to be a half-and-half production of nonsense, partly a poem, partly an acrostic on Augusta's name:

As sweet as the nightingale,
Under the tree,
Gay as a sparrow, perched
Upon your knee;
Singing, ah singing
To me, to me!
Ah, what is he saying to thee?

How can the birdsong
As blithe as the breeze,
Waft on the elements
Kissing the trees,
In sunlight and moonlight,
Night and in morn; the
Sweetest of avians is singing our song.

"Thank you, Mr. Bird, that will quite do. I am very sensible of the honour you do me, but it is quite unnecessary to read me any more such poems."

"Ah, but you do not understand, Miss Hawkins! Have you not noticed the rhyme scheme?"

"I have noticed that I do not have a sparrow perched upon my knee, and upon my word, I don't take in your meaning. Now, Mr. Elton, you do not write poetry, I think?"

"No - certainly not. I do not like the things. A friend of mine once wrote an epigram - a charade - that I borrowed and laid before a young lady; but I was very sorry afterwards that I did, and vowed never to do so again."

"A charade! Before a young lady! That was a dangerous, a rash act, Mr. Elton. I do not dare inquire who was this young lady. How long has she been a favourite?"

"She never was a favourite," he said quietly, "not as I feel now; and if I may say so, Miss Hawkins, my feelings have never been so engaged in my life as - as I suspect the sentiment that may be forming..."

At this interesting moment, with what annoyance did Augusta perceive Mr. Bird's half-whisper breathing into her ear again.

"Miss Hawkins, Miss Hawkins! I believe you did not perceive the meaning of my poem. It is an acrostic. Cannot you see? The first word of every line spells out your name. Augusta Hawkins! There! Do you not like it? Do you not think acrostics very clever things?"

"Insufferable puppy!" said Augusta to Mr. Elton, turning her head and speaking low. "Yes, yes, Mr. Bird - an acrostic. No, I do not think them clever: I believe acrostics are a low form of wit, like a pun."

Mr. Bird was crestfallen. "But Miss Hawkins! It is in honour to you! You do not think I could have written this to any one else, to Miss Milman for instance? You see your name - there - is felicity itself. Philadelphia Milman is far too long. It would never fit."

"I suggest that you try it, however," said Augusta, rising, in response to Mr. and Mrs. Green, who were beginning to collect the party for the procession into the dining-room.

The Compleat Mrs Elton

The Party at Mrs Brown's

I told you," Mrs. Partridge announced to Augusta with satisfaction, "that I would get you married before you was any older; and here you are with two very particular beaux. You need only pick and choose, Miss Hawkins, pick and choose."

"I am very far from knowing what you mean, Mrs Partridge," Augusta answered. "I have had no offers since coming to Bath, although at Maple Grove there are several gentlemen who would be very glad for me to accept any one of their hands; only I am nice in my taste, and not to be so easily suited. To pick a partner in marriage, you know, is not the same as choosing a gown or a ribband, that you can send back again."

Mrs. Partridge and her guest were seated in her drawing room on a sleety February afternoon. No visitors could be expected in such weather; though Mrs. Jeffereys had come to sit with her mother, and the Miss Milmans had struggled through the wet and cold.

"I do hope it will clear before evening," said Miss Milman anxiously, "otherwise we will have a nasty walk in the cold and the dark, to Mrs. Brown's party. It is a great shame we have no carriage of our own."

"Why, Philly, there is always room for you in our carriage, you know very well," said Mrs. Partridge comfortably, "sure we can carry four, since Clara will go in her own. I should think Mr. Cooper would wish to drive his bride-elect, but howsoever, if he does not, you can come with us. And you need not go back to your rooms to dress, you are both fine enough for Mrs. Brown's, as you are; and I can lend you some feathers if you want to rig up a turban or some such fal-lal."

The invitation for the carriage, thus angled for, was accepted, an arrangement that had been made and carried out too often for more words to be wasted upon it. Mr. Cooper would not be going to the party; he had a sore throat, Miss Susan was at some pains to explain. She had begged him to remain at home; and she believed that she had enough influence with him, that it would be so.

"I knew we would be going to Mrs. Brown's tonight, that is why I wore my silk velvet," said Miss Milman, "and I brought the green feathers in my basket. They are not spoiled by the wet at all. Not that it matters what I wear; the gentlemen have no eye for me as they do for Miss Hawkins. Why, at one time, do you know, I suspected that Mr. Bird was positively in love with you."

"He is indeed, and you, Philly, are quite out in the cold," agreed Miss Susan, not without some satisfaction. "Why, he is writing poems to Miss Hawkins! Is it not so, Augusta? And everybody knows that a poem is as good as a proposal."

"Well, if that is so, then we are both engaged to him," said Philadelphia with a toss of her head, "for he has written a poem to me too. An acrostic upon my name. I dare swear it is very clever, for it is much longer than yours, Miss Hawkins. He must have spent much more time on it."

"Naturally, as your name is longer, the poem would be longer," said Augusta with some irritation, "but I told him to do it, so am not surprised he made the attempt."

"And I have learnt it by heart. I can say the sweet words for ever. I shall never tire of them. Could you, yourself, if such were written to you?" And she repeated them:

Perchance your heart, the heart I see
Holds a charming place for me?
I dearly pray that I may find
Love is what you have in mind.
A little love; as by the stream
Dreaming will give way to dream:
Even as the waters flow,
Life slides by, as we all know.
Perchance the remedy for dying,
Happiness never yet expiring,
Is Love: the song that I am sighing.
And so, my loveliest, sweetest maid,

My angel, where my heart is laid,
I implore you, oh, indeed I do,
Love me, sweet, as I love you.
My heart, my hand, my wealth, my name
Are all your own, for you to claim.
Now tell me: is your heart my gain?

There was a silence when she had finished. "It does sound like a proposal," said Mrs. Partridge doubtfully, "but then why does he not follow it up by stating his terms? We have not seen him these three days."

"How can you think that any lines so sacred, could be any thing but a proposal?" said Miss Milman, with some anger.

"Heavens, that is not a proposal, it is a 'Valentine' poem, that is all," observed Mrs. Jeffereys. "Is this not the middle of February? A poem at such a time does not mean anything. Mr. Jeffereys did not propose to me in a poem, I can tell you. He proposed to me in the flesh and told me at once what my clothing allowance would be. It is much better to know than not."

"Is it not possible that he grew carried away with his compliments, as your name is so long?" asked Augusta.

"La! Miss Hawkins, I do believe you are jealous. Mr. Bird would not call my sister an angel, and sweet, and all that, if he did not love her and it was not a proposal. You are only jealous because she will be married before you, and live at that fine house in Kent."

"As to that, Mr. Bird has no fine house; the house in Kent is his brother's, and his income is so very small that he will not be able to afford to marry for many years, if ever. However, you are welcome to him," said Augusta composedly.

Miss Milman subsided in mortification and the ladies sat in what would have been an uncomfortable silence for a few minutes, had they not had the diversion of slapping at Mrs. Partridge's two kittens, which had become miserably entwined in Mrs. Jeffereys' tatting.

"Oh! my lace, it will be spoilt. Mama, I told you to get rid of Euphemia, she is the most insolent cat I have ever seen, without comparison."

"My dear, insolent! It is only her claws, which will get into the tatting if you trail it upon the floor like that. It is positively dangerous. Take care! you will be scratched. Well, I declare, you are being quite cruel to poor Euphemia."

What began to resemble a quarrel between mother, daughter and cats was interrupted by the sound of a carriage that was heard in the street, pulling up before the house.

"Good heaven! somebody coming here! A gentleman, too - why, it is Mr. Elton, I do believe. In this rain! No wonder he has hired a carriage. But what is he about? Clara - Miss Milman, Miss Susan, you had better come upstairs with me. We can sort out the feathers there. I am sure, Miss Milman, that Mr. Bird will like you better in a white feather: you will never win a proposal in green. Come along, come along. Take Euphemia with you, and all the tatting, that's right - Miss Susan, just pick up Sophronia, will you. We must clear the way for the two of them to be alone," she finished, in a whisper. "Oh, yes, very necessary. I am sure he has come particularly on that errand."

Despite Mrs. Partridge's good intentions, Mr. Elton was announced and in the room before the ladies could make their escape. Mrs. Partridge received him with effusive welcomes, and asked if they would have the honour of seeing him at the party at Mrs. Brown's.

"Yes, indeed - to be sure - I had intended to be there. But to say the truth, I called this afternoon on an errand related to this evening. I wonder, in short, Miss Hawkins, if you would do me the favour of reserving for me the first two dances?"

Augusta assented graciously, and Mrs. Partridge made her move. "That is so very gallant of you, Mr. Elton, to come out in all this rain to ask such a question! I hope you will forgive me, therefore, if I am so rude as to - I was just on my way upstairs, to show the Miss Milmans something very particular. Will you excuse me? Will you excuse us all? I am quite ashamed - but Miss Hawkins can entertain you, to be sure."

She tweaked Miss Milman's arm, and grasped Miss Susan by the hand, so that they had no choice but to gather up kittens and fancywork and follow their hostess out of the room. Mrs. Jeffereys, with a resigned air, glided after the other ladies.

Left alone, Augusta found herself blushing. "Mrs. Partridge is very agreeable," she said, "but not always a model of the best breeding. I hope you will excuse her."

"Excuse her? I am grateful to her - I will thank her forever, if the result of this visit is what I have long hoped," exclaimed Mr. Elton, seizing her hand. He thereupon proceeded to present to her nothing less than a very earnest proposal of marriage, to which she listened with as receptive a delight as Mr. Elton himself could wish.

If our lovers were in fact a venial pair, marrying only in a spirit of self-seeking, how much worse were they than half the world? It was such a perfect case of like marrying like, that the most elevated love between two pure souls could be no more perfectly matched. With a strong mutual wish for matrimony, and for each finding a partner who could bring benefits to the other, and a determination and resolve to be bettering themselves, Mr. Elton and Miss Hawkins stood a great chance of finding as lasting a happiness as exists in this mutable world.

In as short a time as could possibly be, the matter was happily settled between them, and when Mrs. Partridge and the other ladies came back down stairs, their arms full of feathers, after a judicious quarter of an hour's absence, they had nothing to do but to set the frippery aside and give Mr. Elton and Miss Hawkins very voluble congratulations.

Mr. Elton and Miss Hawkins danced together for the first time as an engaged couple, that night, at the party at Mrs. Brown's.

The Carriage

*T*he rain blew away; the sun shone; and as the month of March opened to bring daffodils and crocuses to all the gardens of Bath, the happiest couple, because the latest engaged, strolled through Laura Place to Pulteney Street, the lady leaning upon the gentleman's arm. Between the Abbey Churchyard and Milsom Street they planned their household, and on the way to the Pump Room to drink the waters and listen to the music, they talked of the society of the village of Highbury to which Miss Hawkins was shortly to be transplanted. Every thing, in fact, was arranged with the greatest speed and felicity, except one. Mr. Elton had a parish, a house, good furniture, and an income that, with the addition of Miss Hawkins' ten thousand pounds, could never be contemptible; but he did not possess his own carriage.

"I fear, my dear Augusta, that everybody does their carriage-building in preparation for the Spring. I have written to Malone's, and gone to see Sloane and Wilkens, but their hands are full. I do not know what we can do. I wish I had set up a carriage before, indeed; but for a single man, hired hacks sufficed. Yet I cannot bring my bride to Highbury without a carriage."

"To be sure not. But is there no carriage maker - can we not procure the pitifulest old wagon in the world? - I do not ask for a *very* handsome carriage. I do not have pretensions to aspire to a barouche-landau, for of course I know that we will not have the income of my brother Mr. Suckling. For *them*, two carriages are quite a necessary thing."

"No, a barouche-landau, I think, would certainly be out of place in a little country town. Our parishioners would think we were putting on airs."

"Only think! well! how provoking. But I suppose I shall have to accustom myself to having an audience observing everything that we do, and being the cynosure of all eyes. Our choice of carriage will probably be a subject that will make a great stir in Highbury."

"Exactly so, my dear Augusta. We cannot be too careful. Now, curricles are smart; but they do not suit a married couple as well as a landau, I think, or a landaulet would do quite as well."

"Oh, I would not have a curricle for the world. They may do very well for fast young gentlemen, and puppies - Mr. Bird has a curricle I believe - but not for Mr. and Mrs. Elton of Highbury. I am sure you are right, and we should not try to make too smart an appearance; our new neighbours are apt to feel inferior, and I would not have that for a fortune. They are country people, and not used to the elegancies of town, I believe you have told me."

"That is very much the case, my dear. Why, the Woodhouses, and the Bates, and even elegant ladies such as Mrs. Weston and Mrs. Cole, never stir from Highbury. It is different with the gentlemen. Knightley, and Weston, and Cole, sometimes have business that takes them to Town. But they do not mix with the fashionable world. Ah! they will stare to find a lady of fashion, like you, among them, my dear Augusta."

"I shall have to teach them how to do everything, I suppose. I have heard that in these little country places, people dine at four o'clock, and there are no fine parties at all. I am glad you have such a fine cook, and I shall soon have her in the way of making rout-cakes such as we had at the Browns."

"Ah! Augusta, you will civilize Highbury. But the carriage, my dear - the carriage. I confess it seems a desperate business. I begin to fear that we may not be able to set up our carriage, and be married, until *May*, at this rate; and that will be exceedingly inconvenient for my parish, and also for me, as I would wish to be married as soon as can be. You understand, Augusta, and forgive me for being so ardent?"

"Certainly I understand, my dear Mr. E, and your being ardent can only flatter me, you know. When you are my lord and master, I assure you, I shall make a proper return. And I have no fear but that you shall be able to purchase a carriage before many days have passed. Why, any thing can be bought with money; and I am sure, that if we look only a little farther, we shall meet with success. I shall write to Mr. Suckling for advice. Is there not a carriage maker a little out of town, on the London road? Have you applied to him?"

With such encouragement from his lady-to-be, Mr. Elton was not slow in visiting all the carriage-makers in the neighbourhood, and vigorously stating his wishes, until he did meet with success; and for only fifty pounds more than he had hoped to give, he secured his purchase, a shining new landau with a purple silk lining.

So Augusta and Philip were joined in marriage, so early as the first of March. In despite of much conjecture on the point, their wedding was celebrated many weeks before Mr. Bird and Miss Milman were able to agree upon settlements in their own match. A flurry of parties and dinners were given for the Eltons in Bath, in honour of their nuptials, and at every one of these their placid satisfaction was so much in evidence, as to form a contrast with the quarrels between Mr. Bird and his friends, and Miss Milman and hers, each of whom felt the other party was being cheaply dealt with. The truth was, that there was not enough money to go around; if one fortune is all that a couple needs between them, Mr. Bird and Miss Milman were unfortunate in not having any.

Such was not the lot of the happy Eltons, however, and they duly left Bath in their shining new carriage, inaugurating it with a short visit to Maple Grove, in order that Mr. Elton might meet the Sucklings. And so, their courtship having proceeded with incredible swiftness, and their wedding bells rung with celerity, March was not half over, before the newly wedded pair swept into Highbury, and Augusta was settled in the vicarage, with every possible comfort and source of happiness at hand.

Augusta was pleased, on the whole, with everything she saw; the house was good, if small, and new-furnished in the best of modern taste. The servants, she instantly had under command; and everything was soon running with pattern smoothness, as a vicarage ought to do. Mrs. Elton had nothing to wish for, but to take a place in the village society that would be worthy of her position, her income, her husband, and her elegance. Accordingly, on her first Sunday in Highbury, she put on her bridal raiment to make a most elegant and proper appearance in Church, where the wondering townspeople would catch their first glimpse of the vicar's wife, a bride in a pew.

In Defense of Mrs Elton

PART ONE

*A*ugusta Hawkins was neither handsome, clever, nor rich, and had lived five-and-twenty years in the world with a good deal to vex and distress her. Her father and mother had died when she was very young, and the fortune divided between Augusta and her older sister Selina, was so moderate, after her father's dry-goods establishment in Bristol was sold, that it was plain the young women could reasonably look forward to no brilliant or distinguished destiny. Their home with an uncle, an attorney's clerk, was not the home of comfort and plenty: the interest on the girls' portions formed an important part of the household income, and the uncle was a mean, narrow-minded, illiterate man, whose home in the very heart of Bristol was not one calculated to give a young woman any advantage in society.

With the luck that defies prediction in matrimonial affairs, Selina Hawkins, with only so many thousands of pounds as would always be called ten, attracted, in her first season at Bath, the attentions of a young man both rich and liberal, and was rapidly and triumphantly married, while Augusta's lot in life remained to be fixed. It was to be hoped that Selina's triumph would be to her sister's advantage, in being the means of introducing her to other rich young men, but this did not occur: Maple Grove, Mr. Suckling's seat, was certainly all that was luxurious and comfortable, far superior to anything Augusta had ever seen in her straitened Bristol life; but it was in a location very retired, in a small community (as was reflected in the size of the school), so that among all the families the Sucklings visited, there was no eligible young man worthy of the name.

Augusta had, to be sure, a sufficiency to live upon; and she was a welcome guest at Maple Grove, as often as she cared to be there; which, as the place was to her a paradise of peace and plenty, in comparison with her Bristol home, was very often indeed. Maple Grove formed her tastes probably more than it should; and Selina, anxious for her sister, began to give her many hints that it would be well for her to be mistress of such an establishment of her own. As Augusta fully agreed with this, there was nothing for her to do but to visit Bath as often as might be. Her uncle, to be sure, never went into society, and would not make a figure in any circle in Bath that could do his niece any good. Selina could not often be spared from her duties at Maple Grove; and so Augusta was forced into a kind of half-and-half Bath life, making shift with friends married and single, who took young lady guests, and provided the necessary chaperonage to the Rooms and the various private dances and card parties that were so important to a young woman whose object was matrimony.

Eight long seasons did Augusta spend in Bath, without attracting any wished-for Mr. Suckling; and she was in truth growing desperate, if a young lady may ever be said to be desperate, while Selina had given up her chances altogether.

"That girl," she declared, "will never find a husband; she is too nice. I will tell you what, Augusta, you will end as an old maid, indeed you will. You are always very welcome to make your home at Maple Grove, to be sure - very welcome - but I should think you would be too proud, and would try a little harder to do something for yourself."

Three months after Selina uttered these words, Augusta had met a young man who was as anxious to marry her as she could wish to be married; and one month from that date, she was Mrs. Philip Elton, being carried in the ecstasy of her bridal achievement, from her meagre Bath rooms to a new home, a respectable and prosperous vicarage in the Surrey village of Highbury.

The Compleat Mrs Elton

PART TWO

*M*r. Elton was a match, all her friends agreed, beyond any thing that Augusta Hawkins deserved. A young man so handsome, of such unexceptionable character, so universally popular, a clergyman with a good income and a comfortable home - he certainly might have claimed a wife of more than ten thousand pounds; he might have aspired to twenty. In fact, Mr. Elton had aspired to thirty thousand pounds, and had met with such disagreeable mortification in his very unreasonable application, that he had removed himself in no happy temper to Bath, determined not to return to Highbury until he could bring with him a bride that would astonish the place with her style and éclat. In such a mood, he was ready to be caught; and in Miss Hawkins, he found a woman handsome enough, if not an acknowledged beauty, and of fortune useful if not vast. It was, in short, her vivacity, her liveliness of mind and manner, and her extreme willingness to have him, that fixed the matter. Mr. Elton was not a man of more than common manners, and had not discernment enough to know that his bride had not received an education, or mixed in exclusive enough society, for true elegance. She was good-natured, and very well disposed to him; and he found her chat amusing and entertaining. He knew that when he returned to Highbury, he might no longer spend the long winter evenings at Hartfield, as he had been wont to do before the late debacle with the proud, contemptuous heiress, Miss Woodhouse. To have a pleasing, talking young woman like Miss Hawkins as mistress of his home, agreeable and fond of social life as she was, would animate his lonely fireside, and make him happy.

Mr. Elton did not scruple to paint a very agreeable picture of Highbury for his future wife. He feared she would find the village too retired; the society was not extensive. Certainly the vicarage was small, it was nothing at all compared to what she was used to at Maple Grove. The Woodhouses were unfortunately the first family in the neighbourhood, and Mr. Elton anticipated all the social awkwardness that this implied, upon his return. When once Miss Hawkins' affections and promises were engaged, he described to her the families she would soon be intimate with, and on the night following their wedding, that time of all when no secrets need be kept back, he confided to her the whole story of Miss Woodhouse and Miss Smith. The new Mrs. Elton heard it with indignation. Fancy a young woman, with every advantage like that, so rich and so proud, the Queen of her society, daring to look down on her own Mr. E, and treating him as if he were not even a gentleman! And wanting to marry him to her friend - a girl who was not even the product of a legitimate union, the daughter of nobody knew who! Disgraceful. Augusta herself had struggled all her life, had endured more humiliations and rejections in the fine society of Bath than she would care to have admitted. She could feel little sympathy for those who effortlessly reigned over others, and who could even take up a low, baseborn girl on a whim, without fear of social disapproval. Imagine if she, Augusta, tried doing such a thing! She was prepared to hate both Miss Woodhouse - whom her husband had apparently been quite in love with - and Miss Smith, who was absolutely in love with him.

Augusta's only security in her new Highbury life, where she was altogether a stranger, was in the heart and hand of Mr. Elton. It was an unlucky fate that put her down in the very village where lived the woman he had wanted to marry, and the woman who had wanted to marry him, without a hope of their removal from the place. But she was the bride, she was Mrs. Elton; she had achieved the height of her aims and ambitions, and if she was not to be the mistress of an estate like Maple Grove, she might yet be an important, an influential, a useful figure, the great lady of the small village, with only this Miss Woodhouse as a rival. It behooved her, therefore, to make of Miss Woodhouse an ally, for it would be intolerable to be dictated to, for a whole lifetime perhaps, by such a person. As things started out, so they would go on. Together, Mrs. Elton and Miss Woodhouse might run Highbury affairs comfortably between them, and have every thing their own way. They would do so much good! Mrs. Elton prepared for the first meeting with this formidable young lady, with the greatest care and anxiety. It was not too much to say that everything depended upon it.

The Compleat Mrs Elton

PART THREE

*T*he introduction was alarming. Hartfield was a very fine and beautiful old house, of such antiquity and comfort as Mrs. Elton had never seen before in her life; and she could only maintain her composure, and conceal how overwhelmed and unimportant she really felt, by making comparisons with Maple Grove. She knew she was mentioning it too often - she could not help talking too much when she was nervous - and she felt the impression being made upon Miss Woodhouse was an unfortunate one. When she mentioned the staircase at Maple Grove, she distinctly saw a contemptuous expression pass over Miss Woodhouse's proud features. Rattled, she tried to compensate, to overcome the young lady's evident disdain, by throwing a little extra warmth into her manner, and assuming a higher degree of friendship and amity for Miss Woodhouse than she really felt, or than was possible to feel on such short acquaintance. She and Miss Woodhouse must be friends; their situations relative to each other demanded it; and not knowing how to engage so very formidable and proud a young lady, possessed of manners of such icy perfection, Mrs. Elton unwisely chose the unfortunate method of an over-assumption of intimacy. In her anxiety she heard herself suggesting that she and Miss Woodhouse unite to form a musical society - highly desirable and important to Mrs. Elton, to be sure - but it was with chagrin that she saw Miss Woodhouse coldly passing over the suggestion. She tried to present as prepossessing a portrait of herself as she could, impressing upon Miss Woodhouse the position that she, as Miss Hawkins, had held in society; but Miss Woodhouse was not, would not be, impressed. Not by Maple Grove, not by several mentions of her brother-in-law Mr. Suckling's fine carriages, not by her kind offer to introduce her to friends in Bath - what more could she possibly say to appease and engage this young lady?

Augusta knew, even as she was speaking, that everything she was saying was wrong, but she thought that Miss Woodhouse might show some consideration, might feel some sympathy for the uncertainty she felt as a stranger, as a bride. But no sympathy, no warmth was forthcoming. A powerful resentment began to come over Augusta. This Miss Woodhouse was intolerable! Dreadful woman! So self-satisfied, so certain of everything she said! Augusta could hardly keep from putting her down, correcting her when she so arrogantly looked down her nose and declared, "Many counties are called the garden of England, I believe." She argued about everything. Mrs. Elton had not had the advantage of the best music masters, in Bristol, and was thankful to be able to give up the painful obligation to have to play and sing before everybody, at evening parties at Bath as well as before every group of newcomers to Maple Grove. But from Miss Woodhouse's sneers, you would think that giving up music as a married woman, was something reprehensible.

It was plain by the end of a quarter of an hour, that she and Miss Woodhouse were not to be bosom friends. Hopelessly, Augusta tried to impress on Miss Woodhouse that she was to be respected as a married woman, at least; that she had held an important position in society before her marriage; that her sister was well married - but each implied boast, or direct brag, hit the wrong spot, and Miss Woodhouse only looked more and more scornful, if that was possible. Even a compliment spoken about that nice Mrs. Weston, who had been Miss Woodhouse's governess but now had risen to be quite an enviable and important figure in

Highbury society, did not serve. Showing interest and approval of the man who might almost be considered the King of Highbury, Mr. Knightley, an intimate friend of the Woodhouses, did not answer either. Mrs. Elton was hurt, disappointed, at her wits' end. She would have to seek for friends elsewhere, it was very plain. Where could she look? That elegant young Miss Fairfax was more come-at-able, certainly less unpleasing, than this Miss Woodhouse, and might be properly grateful for friendly overtures. Perhaps she would find a friend, an ally, there.

The Compleat Mrs Elton

PART FOUR

*I*njured by the reception she had received from Miss Woodhouse, who refused to treat her either as an equal or as a friend, Mrs. Elton was mollified by the friendly effusions of Miss Bates, whose warmth did something to compensate for the elegant coldness of Miss Woodhouse's manners.

"Very welcome - to be sure, it has quite hurt me that the dear old Vicarage had no mistress - and it is so charming to see our dear Mr. Elton so happy! It is quite a romance. I was telling Jane, that when my dear father was alive, the vicarage was always overflowing. You, my dear, perhaps cannot remember it - I am always forgetting how very young you are, Jane - but our house was so very lively! I know Mrs. Elton will restore it to what it was, and what it ought to be. A vicarage is the heart of a village, you know, quite the heart. The soup we dispensed - I have long been sorry that our circumstances are now too reduced to enable us to carry on that tradition, but when my dear father was here, we were able to be more bountiful, and I shall look out all our good old receipts for you. I believe they are stored in my mother's chest, at least, they used to be. I do not quite like to ask Jane to open it, for she is not strong, but there is no hurry. You will be at the Vicarage a long time, dear Mrs. Elton, and we will find the receipts for you."

Mrs. Elton assented graciously. It was her intention that the Vicarage should be a house of bounty and benevolence, and she asserted that she would by no means suffer anyone in the parish to go hungry.

"Indeed," said she, "I would be sorry if *more* than the poor ever had too little to eat. If you and your mother, Miss

Bates, in your reduced circumstances, should ever require any addition to your diet, I should be only too glad to send over a baking of biscuits, or a chicken. I am quite concerned that Miss Fairfax is not sufficiently nourished. She is so pale and thin, though it is a becoming thinness."

Miss Bates could hardly stop to thank her enough. "Never were such neighbours! But it's quite unnecessary. Dear Mr. Woodhouse lately sent us such a hindquarter of pork - and Mr. Knightley is always so generous with his garden stuff. But you are right about Jane, I cannot persuade her to eat, and sometimes I suspect - I should not say this, but I cannot help suspecting - that some of her meals make their appearance more than once. She cannot always keep her food down."

"How shocking!" exclaimed Mrs. Elton. "We must not allow that to happen. We must take care of you, Jane, indeed we must."

"I am most grateful to you for your concern," said Jane earnestly, "but indeed, I do partake of all that I require; and I have very seldom really been ill. My dear aunt worries about me, but I beg you will not, Mrs. Elton."

"But indeed I shall worry about you, Jane. I knew from the first moment I saw you that we should be the very best of friends; I made up my mind then, that I should visit you every day. You will help me to make my house the perfect vicarage. I can hardly succeed without some hints, for you are a clever creature, I know, and will be an invaluable aide-de-camp, now that I am transplanted and have blossomed into a vicar's wife."

Miss Bates smiled happily. "It will be a privilege to have an interest in the vicarage again, won't it, Jane?" she said. "My mother will be so glad, for old times' sake. It is such a benefit to have proper useful work again."

Jane did not appear to know what to say. "Are you - are you pleased with the house, ma'am?" she asked. "Do you mean to make many changes?"

"It is so very small, that there is not much we can do," replied Mrs. Elton, "other than to throw out a bow or a wing or two, but that will be the work of another year. At present I can only venture to get rid of the yellow curtains, which the housekeeper would inflict upon my poor dear Mr. E. But I do mean to entertain very often, to have card parties and sweet little dinners, in addition to my charitable duties; and you will be my right hand, will not you, Jane?"

Jane said something, which did not carry far, but it was enough encouragement for Mrs. Elton to go on in a confiding vein. "To say the truth, I am aware that my inexperience requires aid - for being the Lady Bountiful of such a parish is quite outside my knowledge - and I did hope to engage Miss Woodhouse as my assistant, as she is so very important in Highbury. But I met with no success in my application."

"So I would imagine," Jane could not help saying.

"Ah! I understand. You are well acquainted with Miss Woodhouse's ways. Of course, you have known her from childhood, have you not? You are quite of an age, and have been visiting in Highbury often."

"Yes, I have always known her."

"Yet I see that you are not intimate. May I ask - forgive me, but is it not your opinion that Miss Woodhouse is a very haughty and proud young lady, above being friends in an ordinary way?"

"You are right, Mrs. Elton, in thinking that we are not intimate friends. I cannot pretend otherwise. We ought to be - and from time to time I have tried; but she has made it very difficult for me to like her, because, to say the truth, I do not believe that she likes me."

"Not like you! Well, Jane, that is very bad - and most inexplicable. You are the person that I like most in Highbury, next to my caro sposo, and so I told him, as soon as ever I saw you. Not to like such an elegant young woman, with such talents, such beauty, and such modesty! I have never seen your equal, not in Bath nor in London neither, and I daresay Miss Woodhouse is jealous. That is it, depend upon it, she is positively jealous."

"Oh! do not run away with such an idea, dear Mrs. Elton," protested Miss Bates. "Miss Woodhouse is such an old friend - and she is so handsome and so rich herself, she could never be jealous of any one, certainly not poor Jane, who has no money you know, and as we suppose, will have to be a governess."

"Such a fate," declared Mrs. Elton positively, "I certainly shall endeavour to spare you. We must find you a husband, as I found my Mr. E.; though I ordinarily despise match-making, I do indeed - I consider it quite vulgar. To be sure, I have heard that Miss Woodhouse prides herself on being an expert, and tries to marry off her friends, but it is not a thing *I* could ever bring myself to do. Indeed, except for introducing my sister to her Mr. Suckling, and the Bragges to one another, I never have. Still, it cannot be denied that a good husband is the very answer for you. What say you to Mr. Knightley?"

"Mr. Knightley!"

"Yes; he likes you. I am sure he does. I observed him the other night when we were at Hartfield. He is at a dangerous age, and when such a man spends so much time looking at a pretty young woman and listening to her sing, I can assure you there is mischief afoot. I have seen a great deal of the world, and understand these matters thoroughly."

"I must beg you not to pursue that line of thinking, Mrs. Elton," said Jane quietly. "Mr. Knightley never has had a thought of me, I am sure, and I do not think of him."

"Oh! well, that's a mistake; he is the only man in Highbury I could accept for you; but if you are determined not to marry, then an eligible situation you must have, and I shall seek one for you. We must not allow you to be lost entirely. If you do not chuse to remain in Highbury, then you must be transplanted to Maple Grove, or its neighbourhood - I have many charming married friends there, you must know. Then I can be sure of seeing you whenever I visit Selina."

"I thank you for your concern, but you are too precipitate, Mrs. Elton, indeed you are. I remain here until the Campbells' return."

"Do you? Well, you know your own interest best, I hope you do; but there is a readiness about me when it comes to business. When I see a thing to be done I do it, and I imagine that this executive turn will serve me well in my vicarage life. Passivity is all very charming, and all that - but not in a married woman." She nodded vigorously. "And so I will do all the work for you, indeed I will. I could do no less for a true friend, and I **am** determined that I shall prove myself a true friend to you."

"Jane will be so obliged," interrupted Miss Bates, "she has never had a real young woman friend in Highbury before, have you, Jane? And where can she look for a more proper friend, than the vicar's wife? We are so obliged, are not we Jane?"

"Yes, we shall be such friends, and no one will recognize Highbury when *we* have done our work together, will they Jane? We shall modernize it entirely. A musical society - a soup kitchen - visits to the poor - card parties - exploring expeditions - a delightful situation as a governess - Oh! only think! what a summer opens before us!"

The Compleat Mrs Elton

PART FIVE

Mrs. Elton's kind attentions to Jane Fairfax had become habit with her, and accordingly she dispatched her carriage to fetch her friend and Miss Bates on the night of the ball at the Crown. She was in great hopes of this ball, for it would introduce her to Mr. Weston's son, Frank Churchill. He would be a new, and it might be, friendly element in the society that was so sternly arrayed against her; and it had not failed to enter her mind that, with some leading from herself, a match between him and Jane might be brought about. Frank Churchill was said to be a very fine young man; and Jane had a heart unattached. She had shown no disposition to try to marry Mr. Knightley, so perhaps Frank Churchill would be the lucky man.

All Mrs. Elton's happy hopes and schemes were doomed, however, by her very early seeing that Frank Churchill did not take to her. She wore lace and pearls, and Wright had spent hours curling her hair into an elaborate arrangement, but Mr. Churchill did not seem to notice her elegant appearance, and only joined with Miss Woodhouse in directing disapproving looks toward the vicar's wife. It could not have been anything she did herself; their acquaintance was not more than ten minutes old, she had only had time to exchange compliments on their dress with Jane, and yet it was plain that he did not like her. He had been told not to like her, by Miss Woodhouse. They talked like intimate friends; probably they had matrimony in mind for themselves: no hopes for Jane there. Mrs. Elton reflected on the consoling thought that the result of a match between Mr. Churchill and

Miss Woodhouse would be the removal of the lady from Highbury. As the new Mrs. Churchill, living at Enscombe, she would be quite out of Mrs. Elton's sphere. It was of all things to be desired.

Mrs. Elton was somewhat cheered by seeing how very much she was the queen of the evening, as a bride had every right to be. She had the honour of opening the ball with Mr. Weston, though it did not escape her notice that Frank Churchill was guilty of some manoeuvring to avoid dancing with *her*. He wanted to dance with Miss Woodhouse instead. Mrs. Elton could excuse that; but she felt evidences of coldness and exclusion everywhere she turned. In the glances exchanged by Mr. Knightley and Miss Woodhouse - by Miss Woodhouse and Miss Smith. They were all her enemies, yet what had she done to any of them? Her ways, her manners, were not like theirs; she knew *that* well enough. She was not capable of their sort of superior insolence, the exquisite politeness that only pointed up the disdain beneath: when she thought a thing, she said it. If they were so petty and exacting as to mind such a difference in her, and disapprove of the manner when the heart was right, what hope had she of ever living in harmony with any of them?

Mrs. Weston, whom Mrs. Elton had never supposed capable of a deliberate unkindness, was the originator of the evening's most uncomfortable moment. Mr. Elton and her husband had privately agreed that he would not dance with Miss Woodhouse or Miss Smith, if he could help it. To be sure, the question of dancing with Miss Woodhouse did not arise; he could be no more eager to avoid the encounter than she was. There came, however, a moment when Harriet was disengaged. Mr. Elton would not ask her to dance. It must be common knowledge to everyone in the room that the girl was still in love with him, he, a married man - only observe how she sat in the corner, making sheep's eyes at him, in a way that everybody must understand. That was how she had goggled at him, several times each day, since long before his marriage. It was only to be expected that Mr. Elton's asking Miss Smith to dance would feature prominently in Highbury gossip. Therefore, to show the Highbury world that he cared nothing for her, he walked about, ostentatiously disengaged. It was then that Mrs. Weston, kindly but with ill-judging interference, directly asked him to dance with Miss Smith!

Mr. Elton caught his wife's eye. He would not pain her for the world, by dancing with a girl so obviously, so embarrassingly, in love with him; and he made some fumbling excuse and backed away from Mrs. Weston. She was mortified, which he regretted, but could not help. Miss Woodhouse had heard and seen the whole thing, and was glaring daggers at them both. For her part, Augusta could not be sorry that her husband had been loyal to her, and she smiled at him, with relief. What was her astonishment, a moment later, when Mr. Knightley himself led Harriet to the set! She understood his action well enough. Mr. Knightley felt sorry for Harriet, and was another of those who disliked Mrs. Elton - influenced by Miss Woodhouse of course - and wished to spite her. She was sorry for it. She had thought better of his good nature.

The Westons, to soothe the ruffled feelings that were fluttering about the room, took special care to invite Mrs. Elton to lead the train into the chamber where the supper was laid. All eyes were upon her as she swept by, and she felt her cheeks burning, but tried to hold her head up with some dignity, and to show herself unconcerned, though she saw Miss Woodhouse's dark, resentful looks upon her the whole time.

Whatever snobberies her neighbours practiced, Mrs. Elton was no faint spirit to be daunted by them, and would not desist in her tries to be liked and accepted by the best society in Highbury. She must live here always; she was fixed to the spot; and in her position as the vicar's wife, it would be most becoming to forgive her enemies. In consequence of such like reflections, she determined that there should be a dinner party, arranged in the proper style; and not many days had passed since the ball at the Crown, before she graciously invited Mr. Knightley, Jane, and Mr. and Mrs. Weston to dine, with the intention of showing that she harboured no ill will to any one. She dared not go so far as to invite Miss Woodhouse, even though there had been a dinner given for her at Hartfield; for she was quite certain that Miss Woodhouse would never accept her invitation.

If Augusta had some lingering hopes of creating an opportunity for an attachment to develop between Mr. Knightley and Jane, her efforts were not met with success. Jane spent the evening sitting by Frank Churchill, who amused her with stories that seemed to be about Ireland, and the Dixon party - Mrs. Elton could not quite catch the sense of it, but Mr. Churchill's mirth was evident, and seemed to give Mr. Knightley much pain. His eyes were often on the young pair, and she could see jealousy written plainly on his features. There could be no doubt that he was in love with Jane Fairfax, and doomed to disappointment.

The dinner carried on like most such occasions; a little flirtation, some indifferent wit, and the most remarkable feature of the evening being Augusta's elaborate piles of exotic fruit, berries and even a pineapple, that she had imported at great expense from London.

PART SIX

*A*s the summer wore on, Mrs. Elton was disappointed by her sister and brother-in-law, who repeatedly put off their visit to Highbury, and she began to have unhappy thoughts about their refusals. She knew she had not married as high as Selina, but she had hoped her sister would want to make an early visit to inspect her happiness; and there could be no doubt that the arrival of the prosperous couple in their barouche-landau would have been of assistance in improving Augusta's own standing in Highbury. But the Sucklings did not come. Was Selina ashamed that Augusta was only a clergyman's wife? The Sucklings had seemed to approve of the match, but perhaps it was only that they thought she was old enough to catch at any thing. Yet Mr. E. was not any thing - he was the best husband in all the world, as Selina should have seen for herself when they made their wedding trip to Maple Grove. Augusta would have enjoyed showing her Highbury and showing Highbury the famous Mrs. Suckling.

It was not to be. A restless summer lay ahead, without any schemes of happiness, and Augusta daily felt more uneasy and out of things. This would never do; some attempt toward cheerfulness must be made. She proposed the plan of a drive to Box Hill; but was only rewarded by the mortification of understanding that Miss Woodhouse was so little disposed to join her party, that she insisted on undertaking a separate trip of her own. Mr. Weston, however, was ever Mrs. Elton's kind friend, if nobody else was; and he, with his good heart and social manner, brought about a joining of the two parties. They were all to go together. Miss Woodhouse could not excuse herself without extreme awkwardness, and embarrassing the Westons.

In the event, the party had to be put off; but Mrs. Elton's excessive disappointment was completely done away with by Mr. Knightley's good-natured proposal that they all come to Donwell to eat his strawberries. She seized at this suggestion with delight. Perhaps he did like her, after all! She had always thought he honestly did, that it was his nature to be benevolent and kind-hearted, and that it was only Miss Woodhouse who poisoned him with her own dislike. It was beyond doubt that the strawberry-party was made for her; and her spirits rose at the prospect, even to a pitch a little too high. She pictured herself at last, in her excitement, as all she had ever dreamed of being in Highbury: the Lady Patroness, the inviter of all guests, the bringer of Jane Fairfax. If Mr. Knightley reproved her mildly, he did not rescind the invitation, and Mrs. Elton checked herself, aware that she had been a little too eager. It was her way to be vivacious, it was her love of life. To show that she had no resentment, she warmly assured Mr. Knightley that she had no objection to meeting Miss Woodhouse, and she even offered him the use of her housekeeper.

The day dawned with perfect Midsummer beauty. Donwell was lovelier than Mrs. Elton could have conceived, with its ripening berries, and sweet views; and best of all she had received tidings that morning of the very situation she had been seeking for Jane. Her friend Mrs. Smallridge was in want of a governess. She instantly laid the good news before Jane, but Jane was in no good humour. It was understandable; she could not rejoice in the reality that she must be a governess after all. And today of all days, her fate would seem harder than ever, placed as she was in such a setting as Donwell, regarding Mr. Knightley's verdant fields and the mellow, handsome old Abbey. She, who might have chosen to be mistress of Donwell, would be cast off from good society forever. Mrs. Elton was sorry for her, but really the girl must face facts: with all her loveliness, and with every virtue and talent in the world besides, she had no money. If she would not seek a great match, then she must accept the consequence. There was no other choice. The Campbells must have thrown her off; and to remain in the penury and squalor of the Bates' upstairs apartment for month after month, was no answer. Yes, it was time for her to be practical, and accept what must be.

But Jane would not acquiesce, she would not see reason, she would not accept the situation with Mrs. Smallridge at once, and when Mrs. Elton, with the determination of a forceful nature, persisted in importuning her, she impetuously walked away from Donwell, declaring - to Miss Woodhouse, of all people! - that she was fatigued. Fatigued! There was that spirit of independence about Jane, that was too ridiculous. Mrs. Elton truly wished to help her, and knew what was for her own good; why then must the girl be walking all over the countryside on a hot day, agitating herself? She gave it up. Some people are more unreasonable, the more you try to do for them.

Frank Churchill arrived from Richmond late in the afternoon, and accepted the invitation to join the party to Box Hill, which was to take place on the following day. That day was less festive than the previous one. There was a long and tiresome drive to get through, before Box Hill could be reached; and upon arrival, everyone seemed out of sorts. Mr. and Mrs. Elton's best attempts to be sociable, went for nothing. Mr. Knightley walked with Jane and Miss Bates, and seemed to veer away whenever Augusta approached, though she was sure she could have done nothing to offend him yesterday, and was truly grateful for the memory of the Donwell party, as she told him over and over again. Was it her manner again, her unfortunate manner? Why was it that these people would never hear the good sense and intention of what she was saying, and be more generous in their assessment of her address? Mr. Churchill walked apart with Miss Woodhouse and Miss Smith. They put their noses up in the air and would not allow her to come near them, though Mrs. Elton was as ready as anybody could possibly be, to let bygones be bygones.

When they all came to sit down, it was Mrs. Elton's time to be positively shocked at the rate at which Mr. Churchill and Miss Woodhouse went on together. They must have a private understanding; such intimate chat and flirtation could only be permissible between an engaged couple. Augusta had never talked to Mr. Elton with such freedom, before their engagement. Mr. Churchill all but declared his love openly, before them all - and Miss Woodhouse encouraged him with the most blatant, the most insolent complacence. What did the girl think she was, the queen of Box Hill as well as of Highbury, the queen of everybody's hearts? Why oh why was it that nobody saw through Miss Woodhouse, but Mrs. Elton? No, Miss Woodhouse was always the standard of perfection it seemed, no matter how shocking her behaviour. The crowning evidence of this was in the very joke Mr. Weston so gallantly made, calling "perfection" M and A - Emma.

To turn aside this sort of insufferable pleasantry, Mrs. Elton was forced to absolutely protest Mr. Churchill's and Miss Woodhouse's rude demand to hear what everybody was thinking of. How dared they ask such a thing? If Mrs. Elton really told them what she was thinking of, they would be shocked and sorry enough. She wished she could. She had never in her life witnessed such self-centred, arrogant behaviour as theirs. She was disgusted in every particular.

At the last, not content with offensive joking, Miss Woodhouse even stooped to make poor Miss Bates the target of her cruel taunts. This was a kind of poor taste that Mrs. Elton found infinitely distressing, as everyone must, who had a heart. Poor Miss Bates - as tiresome as she could be, it was a wicked thing to make unkind jests at one so poor, so harmless, so kind. Bristling, Mrs. Elton had had enough, and showed that she had. Her husband instantly proposed that they walk, and she was relieved to rise and take his arm. They moved away, but not so quickly that they did not collect that Frank Churchill was embarking on some very unkind remarks upon them as a couple.

"Oh Philip," said Augusta, in misery, "what is it? Have we not tried every thing? - but it is a complete failure. You were popular and happy in Highbury before I came, I know, but instead of being a helpmeet, and making your life easier, I have only brought you trouble. They all hate me - I know they do. Miss Woodhouse, Knightley, Frank Churchill. You will never be comfortable again, and it is all my doing. I have only tried to be friendly. Perhaps my city ways are not what they are used to in a country village."

"Do not distress yourself, Augusta," said her husband tenderly. "You are imagining things. I have been a thousand times happier since we were married; a million. No one dislikes you. There is no pleasing Miss Woodhouse, you know - I could not do it myself, long before I ever met you; and the animosity between us had its origins in nothing to do with you. And that proud young lady leads all the others. But I feel sure that in time they will come to appreciate your real goodness, as I do. To my mind, the whole town should be in love with you, and I do not believe they are not."

Mrs. Elton laughed a little, and leaned on him affectionately. "You do make me feel better, Philip. When I am in my right mind, I know very well it is just Miss

Woodhouse's dislike that causes all the trouble. Have you ever heard anything like her insolent talk? She is the most unladylike young woman that I ever saw."

"Exactly so, my dear," he replied, "exactly so. But she will get her comeuppance in the end, and be taught the error of her ways, you may depend upon it."

PART SEVEN

*M*rs. Elton's most exclusive circle of friends was straitened, and reduced of much of its sense and intelligence, by the loss of Jane Fairfax, that followed as the almost immediate result of her engagement. It was a loss so considerable, so complete, that Mrs. Elton only became sensible of its scope and irreparability, after it was accomplished. No other acquaintance of hers had Jane's refinement, her sensibility, her elegance. Mrs. Cole, Miss Bates, Mrs. Goddard - how were they to be compared to a Jane Fairfax? But Jane was gone, and gone for ever; she had first gone to London with the Campbells, and at last into Yorkshire with her husband and gone happily, without a backward look or remembrance of old friends, as far as Augusta could see. It was a certainty that she only would appear again in Highbury on fleeting visits to her grandmother and aunt, and at such times it was not to be expected that Mr. Frank Churchill would allow his wife much leisure for visiting with Mrs. Elton, whom he cordially disliked. The friendship would sink. In sober sadness, it had never recovered from the very moment of the astonishing, the tremendous revelation that Jane and Mr. Frank Churchill had long been secretly engaged.

Mrs. Elton had been disappointed - very disappointed. It was not that she did not rejoice in Jane's good fortune, in her escape from a life of servitude; every good friend must rejoice in that; but the idea rankled, that Jane had kept a secret of such magnitude from one who had supposed herself her dearest friend. No: Augusta's hurt feelings were all a result of the knowledge breaking in on her that the girl whom she had patronized, brought forward, done endless favours for, planned for, soothed, and loved, that this person could care so little for her as to be always enacting a lie, the very same lie she acted before the most indifferent people, indeed to the world at large. Surely she could have made a confidante of Mrs. Elton, if no one else - a married woman, older and wiser, as she was. Perhaps she might not, as it was a matter of honour; but with honour, Jane Fairfax seemed to have had very little to do. At the very least, however, she might have given a hint, so that Mrs. Elton might not be so humiliated in the eyes of the world. How must she look to Mrs. Smallridge, and to Selina, too! Offering up the pearl of all governesses, backing Jane with her word, her reputation, her judgement; and then having to take back the offer in such a way as to show that she had never really known this Jane Fairfax at all?

To be sure, Jane had made an apology of a sort; but it was so triumphant, so careless an apology as to sound more like a rebuke. Her attentions to Mrs. Elton had ceased the instant Frank Churchill appeared to publicly take charge of her, and Mrs. Elton was left with most wounded feelings, and a sure knowledge that she had only been used. Jane's so-called, much-vaunted friendship, was only a deliberate deceit, a ruse to keep others from suspecting the real state of affairs with regard to Frank Churchill. That was how much Jane Fairfax had cared for Augusta Elton. Mrs. Elton's vanity, of which she was sensible she possessed a great deal, was stung to the quick. She had judged Jane to be the fairest of true, grateful friends; and she had been wrong. She had loved her, and not been loved in return - she had not even been respected. Augusta was within a moment of reflecting pensively on what quality in her own character, failed to win her the love of those whose love she sought. She turned over in her mind poetry associated with the thought..."They flee from me that sometime me did seek"... Then came the more fortunate recollection of Mr. Elton, and she was at once buoyed up and reassured. There, she had wished to attach, and she had attached him. What was more, they had expectations of another to love; and as a wife, the mistress of a vicarage, and a mother to be, Mrs. Elton would soon be too busy and too important to seek female friendship.

Yet whenever she did think of Jane, she must be troubled, irritated, hurt. It had been her unpleasant duty to write to Mrs. Smallridge and acquaint her with her misfortune; a letter written in humiliation, anger, and chagrin. The frustration of all her well-meant, well-laid plans in that direction was hard to bear. She had acted with such a complete and certain sense of what would be best for Jane! She had argued, she had forced her opinion, she had been even peremptory, all for Jane's benefit. Even Miss Bates knew the worth of what she had done - had she not called her the best, most far seeing, indefatigable, true friend to Jane, for not admitting a denial about Mrs. Smallridge: those words had formed part of her apology to the vicar's wife. Miss Bates, at least, had tried to smooth over the hurt feelings that Augusta betrayed, and the indifference, the callous, joyous indifference to them, that Jane herself made only too plain.

Jane had left Highbury, recovered, blithe, and rich; and Augusta remained, to reflect on her own bitterness and failure. She had been eight months transplanted to Highbury, eight months had elapsed from her own wedding day to Jane's; and what had been accomplished, what learned in that time? She had established a happy marriage, that could not been disputed, and she had made some, if not many, friends. But she, who had always prided herself on her clear thinking, her capability, her judgment of character, her management of affairs - she was so shaken in her estimate of herself, as to be closer to a depression of spirits than she had ever known since her marriage. Was it wrong to be a do-all, to try to arrange other people's lives, in the name of helping them, or was it really a vanity-bait for one's own imagined talents? She saw a resemblance to Mrs. Knightley in herself in this way, and she did not like it. Now that she was to be a mother, Augusta reflected, she would have to be more sober, more staid, more sensible.

PART EIGHT
Not the conclusion yet

iss Woodhouse had held a position in Highbury society, that could only be surpassed by Mrs. Knightley. At not yet two and twenty, to be the mistress of both Hartfield and Donwell, and of the combined fortunes of both the Woodhouse and Knightley families, would be called an enviable situation by almost anybody; and Mrs. Elton did envy it. She had known how it would be from the first. Miss Woodhouse had disliked her so much, that she could expect no love from her in her married state; and to be excluded from every thing desirable that might be going on in Highbury, was all that Mrs. Elton expected. She knew she had acted unwisely in her treatment of Jane Fairfax, and that she had got off on the wrong foot with Miss Woodhouse; nothing could be clearer. She had been made sensible, by the reserve and coldness she had met with, that her manners were not those of the Highbury set that Mrs. Knightley deemed to be the best and the chosen. She repented; she was sorry for her presumptuous, vain behaviour, and for whatever in her own address was not acceptable to others. What could she do? It was rather late in life to become meek and retiring, to go about in a close bonnet ministering to the poor, and giving up all the fun of a really first rate card party.

She had always prided herself on her resources, but the truer knowledge of herself that she had gained in this past year, showed her that she was a person who loved society, who could not do without intercourse with her fellow beings; and to be hated by all those around her, was to a person of

Augusta's temper the worst fate imaginable. She held this fate, the condition that was to be her future, in gloomy contemplation. To be sent to Coventry in Highbury: a heavy conclusion for one who had spent whole seasons in the gay world of Bath and Bristol.

She had reckoned, however, without Mr. Knightley and his influence. His fairness of mind, and true good nature, would not rest easy in allowing the social persecution of the vicar and his wife, however his own wife might wish to institute such a system of proceeding. That Mr. Knightley's good nature was even increased since his marriage, could not be doubted by any observer, not even by the critical Mrs. Elton. She had early calculated that there would be an end to all visiting, and it was true enough that the bachelor Knightley could come no more; but to her infinite surprise (as almost all of life is a surprise), Augusta found that the Knightleys did visit the Eltons, and even invited the Eltons, at intervals, to visit them. On all such occasions, to be sure, the doting husband was to be seen beaming rather foolishly at his beautiful young wife, and attending to very little else; but the toleration of this was a tax easily paid.

It was during the round of wedding visits that the Eltons were first astonished by the spectacle of the newly married Knightleys seated happily at the vicarage dinner-table, a place Miss Woodhouse had always disdained. It is true, nothing very sensible was said on the occasion; the happy couple was so absorbed in one another they had, as the saying goes, no eyes for any one else, though they were unaware of it, and considered that they were behaving as politely as before Hymen had tied her silken strands. It was delight enough for Mrs. Elton, to have these guests in her house, to show the Highbury world that she was of the elite circle, after all.

In Defense of Mrs Elton

She was thankful that the state of affairs between her and Mrs. Knightley seemed to be mending, as was highly desirable, not only because Mr. Knightley and Mr. Elton were mutually involved in a thousand parish matters, but because the two ladies perforce must also be thrown together, like it or not. After all, there were not many married women in Highbury Mr. Knightley could visit - one could think if she could be happy strolling down to the Martins' farmhouse now, for a talk about the cows with Harriet. Mrs. Knightley and Mrs. Elton had got off to a bad start, and they must try again: their husbands were united on this point. They must agree to tolerate one another's ways, and within a few months, both were grown so hardened to meetings by chance or by design in the daily wayfaring life of Highbury, as not to give their prejudices more weight than was absolutely necessary.

Change, however, was in the air. First came the momentous event, the birth of Mrs. Elton's child. Her caro bambino was, she was sure, the finest little boy ever born in Highbury; Mr. Perry said so, and he was a judge. All the world must come to inspect little Philip Augustus, and Mr. and Mrs. Elton were so very delighted, and so hospitable in greeting all comers, and inviting them to partake of seedcake and port, that the good feeling Mr. Elton had brought to Highbury with the announcement of his marriage, seemed positively to revive.

The second great event of the new year, was the long-awaited visit of the Sucklings. It being the depths of winter, and not the more open season of summer, exploring-parties in the barouche-landau were prohibited; but Mrs. Elton did not now have a regret. It was in a most exulting state that she prepared to show her house, her husband, her child, her society, to her most beloved sister, Selina.

The Compleat Mrs Elton

PART NINE

Still not the conclusion

"My dear Mr. Knightley," said his wife, "I am resigned to the daily display of a sort of good fellowship with Mrs. Elton, as it tends to our living in peace together; but really this is going too far. Tell me we do not have to invite her sister to Hartfield, that the name of diplomacy does not demand such a thing."

"My beloved Emma," her husband replied, "you answer your own question. In a community life, diplomacy is always required; and we can hardly show friendship to Mrs. Elton, and not to her sister. This visit, as you know, is very important to her, and in all probability, will never recur again."

Emma threw a despairing look at her friend. "Mrs. Weston, surely you do not agree with my husband? You have never given in to Mrs. Elton's good nature - you still consider her a designing, petty, presuming, interfering little woman, do you not, with her caro sposo, and now her caro bambino, and all her airs?"

Mrs. Weston's eyes were on her little Anna, who at eight months old was attempting to creep forward on a blanket laid upon the floor. Mr. Weston was down on the floor himself, overseeing the child's progress. Such was the disarray at Randalls since the birth of the little household tyrant.

"I do not know - oh, Mr. Weston, she must not eat the blanket, do take it away from her - it is dirty, quite dirty."

"Nonsense! who was it said a child must eat a pound of dirt in its first year."

"She shall not eat it all at once, while I look on, Mr. Weston. Here, my precious, come to mamma."

"Do not let the child eat any thing dirty, Mrs. Weston," said Mr. Woodhouse anxiously, "and I am very glad you have picked her up. It is very chilly on the floor, I know. My own feet are resting upon the floor, and I feel the draught passing over them. I do indeed. She is much better upon your lap."

"But Mrs. Suckling," said Emma impatiently, "what about Mrs. Suckling."

"Oh - well, Emma, she is not my first favourite person, as you know, but I confess that I must incline toward Mr. Knightley's view. It would never do to offend her. I know your good nature will accept the truth of this. Is my love hungry? Perhaps we may give her some of the milk pudding that you have recommended, Mr. Woodhouse, now."

"I do not recommend most solid food for the first year of life," he replied, "indeed, poor Isabella and poor Emma did not take any thing thicker than pudding for the first two years, if I recall aright - and then gruel, a nice thin gruel, may be taken. But I think your little Anna is not quite ready for that yet. She has only two teeth. The greatest care must be taken of her teeth, you know. Babies are delicate plants, especially young lady babies."

"That's a consideration," cried Mr. Weston. "I am sure little Anna will like some of Mr. Woodhouse's good gruel when she is old enough. But you were talking about the Sucklings, Emma. I hope you will invite them to Hartfield; we will have them to Randalls, will we not, my dear? In the winter, at such times as these, good company, good fires, good cheer, and plenty of it, is what is needed to help us all on."

"There, you see, Emma," said Mr. Knightley with a smile, "you are out voted. But do not dread the event. With your interest in studying human nature, Mrs. Suckling will be sure to afford you a new subject. You know you will be talking of her and thinking of her, and so she will be a new source of pleasure, in one sense."

"Very well," said Emma with a sigh, "I shall send out my cards, and we will have a full dinner, in state, for the Sucklings. I am sure they will be horrible in every way."

The Compleat Mrs Elton

PART TEN

*I*t was a very great event, that a dinner for as many as ten people should be given at Hartfield on a dark and early February evening, but all the invitations were accepted, and the Eltons, the Sucklings, and the Westons, as well as Miss Bates, joined the Knightleys and Mr. Woodhouse, in being seated around a table with sufficient abundance and variety of food placed upon it, as to make Mr. Woodhouse very uneasy.

"Upon my word," said Miss Bates, "this is quite - I never saw a more brilliant table, Mrs. Knightley. Goose, and pheasants, and such a pudding of larks! Goodness me! Did you ever see the like, Mrs. Weston? You, Mrs. Suckling, used as you are to great spreads, may not be surprised at the sight, but I assure you, living in such a small way as I do, I am quite overcome. But no one ever had such neighbours - shall I really have some of the goose's breast, Mr. Woodhouse? and juniper berry sauce? Do you not consider it too rich?"

"Indeed I do think goose is a meat no stomach can bear," said Mr. Woodhouse, "and I would advise you to satisfy yourself, as I do, with plainer fare. The bread pudding, I think, could not harm you. Mrs. Suckling, we are honoured by your presence in this house, and I wish you to be as comfortable as possible. But I do not recommend the goose to you either, or to any body." Mrs. Suckling, a little woman with a sharp face and a very large feathered headdress, looked at him with some respect.

"Thank you for your concern, sir. My sister has told me of your great solicitude for the health of your guests, Mr. Woodhouse, and what a kind gentleman you are. Quite a worthy after my own heart. Indeed, I will follow your advice, for I never eat rich food, and very little meat at all. I prefer to eat only greens, and pulse, and a little fish."

"Is that so, Mrs. Suckling?" said Mr. Weston in wonderment, "and does this resolve proceed from a concern for your health?"

"It proceeds from a concern for every body's health, Mr. Weston," she replied, "it can be of no benefit to any one, to eat animals."

"My wife is a very fine lady," spoke up Mr. Suckling, a tall gentleman with a sarcastic expression, "ordinary food is too coarse for her, and she exists upon mere air."

"But that is so very strange!" exclaimed Miss Bates. "You resemble Jane in that - my niece Jane - Mrs. Elton will have told you all about her. Mrs. Churchill, as she is now, I should say. The most delicate appetite that any lady ever had. While she was here, I could hardly get her to take half an ounce of meat, and six to one it would reappear again - though I should not say that - Jane would not like me to say that. But I assure you she grew so thin, I was quite terrified. I hope her husband, Mr. Frank Churchill, will have better luck in making her take her food properly. It is sad to see a young woman with no appetite. I like to see a young person with a bit of flesh about her. Mrs. Knightley likes to eat - Mrs. Weston does - so do we all - all except Jane - "

"I hope Mrs. Suckling will take just what she likes," exclaimed Emma, to cut Miss Bates off a little; and she attempted a change of subject. "Now that you have seen Surrey, Mrs. Suckling, how do you like this part of the country? - You cannot see many of our most striking views at this time of year, to be sure, but I hope the neighbourhood around Highbury pleases you."

"I have seen it before, in more favourable seasons, Mrs. Knightley; my sister may have told you about our exploring parties, and we have travelled very widely in all parts of England. Indeed, it was our extensive journeying that has made it necessary to delay our engagements in Highbury. We have this year travelled to Dorset - to the Lakes - to Yorkshire - to Birmingham - to London, and back again, more than once."

"She hates travelling," put in Mr. Suckling, "and it is a misery to go any where with her."

"Do not joke, my love; you know I always accompany my lord and master wherever you journey, and I make very little complaint, I assure you."

"No - you do not complain; but the degree of commotion you make about having the right sheets, and not eating any animal food, and about the draughts, and the gait of the different horses, is scarcely to be conceived. It is enough to drive one mad. Did our business, and social engagements, not require it, I should never stir from home."

"And what is your business, sir?" asked Mr. Knightley with interest. "Forgive me, but we have never heard."

"Sugar, my good sir, sugar. My plantations in the West Indies are extensive, but business cannot look after itself, and it is necessary for me to travel the country, up and down, to all four corners, in order to assure myself of the best trade."

"And does your business require that you visit the West Indies?" asked Mr. Weston curiously.

"No, no, I leave that part of the concern in the hands of others - a man cannot be everywhere at once, and I have people who can be trusted to look after my property in the West Indies, and deal with the plantations, and the rebellions, and the overseers, and the absurd death rate, and things of that nature. But we must not be distressing the ladies. Ladies do not have a head for business, you know, sir. They take on about every least thing."

"Oh, my dear brother," interjected Mrs. Elton eagerly, "I beg you should not say such a thing about ladies. Ladies are quite as capable as gentlemen: they are indeed. I always take the part of women, at every opportunity, and I am convinced that some day, women will be quite as good at business as men. I am sure I have a fine head for business, have I not, Mr. Elton? Is it not so?"

"Exactly so, my love; better than mine, truth be told. You are the business woman in our family. I do not care about it so much as you do."

"No more do I," put in Mr. Woodhouse. "Our family made its fortune so long ago, that I have never had to know any thing about it. It is very lucky. I am very glad of it. I should not like to be such a man of incessant action as you are obliged to be, sir. And I hope you will be very comfortable while you are here, and take some of our good broth, if nothing else - our broth is perfectly clear, you see, with not a speck of any thing in it, boiled just as Serle knows how to do. It is really not much stronger than water. It will settle your stomach after the hardships of your travels, I am sure."

"The sugar business!" exclaimed Emma, when her father had stopped speaking. "I am sure, Mr. Suckling, that Mrs. Elton has told us that you were a friend to the abolition. Yet you seem to imply that slaves are employed in your business."

"Certainly," he replied calmly, "I would wish to abolish the slave trade, a degrading business; but those who are already slaves, may doubtless be used with impunity. However, ladies do not understand these things."

"My dear brother, there is no limit to what ladies understand - "

"That's true - very true," said Mr. Knightley hastily, "no one wants to discuss trade at dinner. So, Mrs. Suckling, this is your first visit to Hartfield. Do you find it much like your own home, Maple Grove, of which we have heard so much? Mrs. Elton has told us that you would say so."

"Nothing like it at all," said Mrs. Suckling. "No resemblance. Maple Grove is much larger - and much more retired. Augusta, how could you say such a thing?"

"Why, Selina, the staircase - and the garden grouping - you know it is like Maple Grove in those respects."

"Only as much as any great house is like any other. But your own house is so small, my dear Augusta, that you are no judge. You have grown accustomed to living in little rooms."

Mrs. Elton was silenced.

"Oh, Mrs. Suckling, do you think the Vicarage is small?" said Miss Bates. "If I may be allowed to contradict you, I do not think it so *very* small. It was always adequate for our needs, when we lived there; and now that Mr. and Mrs. Elton have a family, they may enlarge it perhaps, and make improvements."

"Another year," said Mr. Elton, "and we shall make an addition. Do you not recommend it, Mr. Suckling?"

"Whatever you like," he said indifferently, "you cannot expect to be able to afford to do much, with your present income. I have told you, Elton, that you ought to come into business with me. Sugar is the thing. That is where the money is."

"It is very tempting, my dear sir - but a clergyman - the West Indies - slaves - it is perhaps not compatible with the duty I owe to my parish."

"Such scruples are absurd. How do you suppose I can afford to give my Selina her barouche-landau, and all the luxuries of Maple Grove, were it not for sugar? We are not of an old landed family, you know, and must do the best we can for ourselves. A clergyman, in these days, is not expected to starve himself in the name of duty."

"And you must remember, Augusta, that howsoever rich we may be, we cannot be expected to help you, should you grow impoverished; for we have a family of our own, and all our money must go to our dear children," said Mrs. Suckling, nodding vehemently until her feathered headdress shook.

"I should not think of anything else, sister," said Mrs. Elton, rather offended, and not knowing where to look to hide her embarrassment.

Emma, amazed by the real vulgarity and heartlessness of such a discussion at her own dinner-table, lifted her eyes expressively. Mr. Knightley seemed to feel her distress, as well as his own, and he proposed that the gentlemen should sit apart with their port, with rather more alacrity than ordinarily was his custom.

PART ELEVEN
Conclusion at last

he Sucklings were gone from Highbury, and nobody was sorry to see them go, or regretted them when they were gone. Mrs. Suckling's selfishness and haughtiness, not to mention the shocking revelation of her husband's involvement in a low business, had not won friends for them among those in Highbury whom they had visited. However, there was one result of their visit which might not have been expected: it was that they left behind them a new feeling of pity for Mrs. Elton, in Mrs. Knightley's bosom.

It was absolutely necessary, after that momentous dinner party, for her to talk it over with Mrs. Weston; and for once Emma found her friend tolerably disengaged, for the baby was asleep, and Mr. Weston was not at home. "I never would have believed it, Mrs. Weston," Emma began, "that I should actually feel sorry for Mrs. Elton. Never would I have thought it possible to entertain such a sentiment."

"It is very natural, Emma," said her friend, "the Eltons may have their little imperfections, but the Sucklings seem far less amiable."

"Less amiable! Far, far too weak a word. Oh, Mrs. Weston, did you not perceive that Mrs. Suckling is a cold hearted woman, who cares nothing for her sister, and disdains every body else; she is a fit wife for a man who persecutes slaves, and admits it!"

"Persecute, Emma! I must think your language is too strong. Would you like Mr. Suckling better if he did not admit his practices? But his conduct, in speaking of such matters at the dinner table, and before ladies, was certainly most improper."

"Improper! he is so very opposite to all that a gentleman should be, that I think we may take exception with any one who calls him a gentleman at all. Poor Mrs. Elton, to have such connections, and to be treated so shabbily by them. I wonder how she will talk of her dear sister Selina now - if she will dare ever mention her again, now that the veil has been removed from our eyes, and we all know what she is. I confess that I shall not be sorry to have heard the last of Maple Grove."

"Maple Grove - and Jane! Only think, my Emma, what a narrow escape Jane Fairfax has had. What if she had gone to the Sucklings' friends as governess, and found herself settled in such a society as that? Dear, dear. I hate to think of it."

"Well, you do not need to think of it; Mrs. Frank Churchill is safe, quite safe. I tell you what, Mrs. Weston, I have made a resolution, and it is that in future, I shall be kinder to Mrs. Elton."

Mrs. Weston smiled gently, and looked up from the infant's dress she was embroidering. "I do not think you will regret it, my dear Emma," she said wisely.

The new friendship of Mrs. Knightley and Mrs. Elton could not be said to leap ahead into any remarkable intimacy. It did not proceed with the youthful rapidity of Emma's infatuation for Harriet Smith, or Mrs. Elton's own with Jane Fairfax. They were older, wiser, soberer women now, who had learned to judge their neighbours better, and to move more cautiously. But they worked amicably on parish affairs, visited the cottages of the poor together, and as Emma remained unpersuadable on the subject of card parties, they finally did unite, after all, to form a musical society, an institution that brought the greatest of pleasure and satisfaction to them both. Mrs. Elton had neglected her instrument shamefully since her marriage; but so had Mrs. Knightley, and neither was therefore in any danger of outdoing the other's musical or vocal performance in any alarming way. Emma was quite certain that Augusta's skill on the pianoforte was comfortably inferior to her own; and Augusta thought that her own performance was just so superior, as to be in no danger of any challenge from Emma.

Music, though a pleasant diversion, could not be as important or prominent in the lives of the two young women as their own growing families; for it was less than a year after the birth of Mrs. Elton's caro bambino, that Mrs. Knightley, too, gave birth to a son, quite as stout and healthy as Mrs. Elton's own child. And so, apart from the disputations that arose over which lady would receive precedence in all the drawing rooms of Highbury, and the resentment that occasionally arose in Augusta's bosom when she felt her husband was not held in sufficient esteem by Knightley, and the jealousies that were uncovered whenever Mrs. Frank Churchill made a visit and was in demand simultaneously at Hartfield and the vicarage - apart from these little differences, and conflicts, and rubs, there was no end to the perfect happiness and amity in which they all lived together.

The Compleat Mrs Elton

MRS ELTON IN AMERICA

CHAPTER ONE

Mrs. Elton always wished to be going somewhere. By the time she had been ten years married, the little fit of restlessness that was habitual with her, had risen to a storm. Nothing would do, she thought, but a tour to the Alps - or a sail upon the Mediterranean - or an exploring party to Italy. On the whole, that country held the most attractions for Mrs. Elton: many great ladies, she knew, had journeyed to Rome and to Florence and brought back statues; and of all things, she longed to emulate their example. A preserve of statues would look well in the Vicarage garden.

Want, as is too usual in such cases, would have to be her master; for he who was her master, in fact and in deed, would not budge. Unlike his wife, Mr. Elton did not want to be travelling. Why should he? England, in his opinion, was the very finest country in the world, and had the finest towns; and of them all, what could be finer than Highbury? Then, of all houses in Highbury, the vicarage, improved as it had been over the years of Mr. Elton's incumbency, was now one of the very finest of all. It had been hardly habitable when first he came into possession - very nearly a ruin - but with the labour of several succeeding summers, and considerable of the money his wife had brought into the marriage, much had been done. The house had been brought to sit farther back from the road. This measure had been rendered necessary by the increase in the movement of traffic in and out of Highbury in recent years, for wagons and chariots went by with such frequency now-a-days, even on quiet Vicarage Lane, as to be quite a nuisance. The new placement, setting the house amongst its own lawns and shrubbery, gave it a look of more consequence. It followed that a carriage-sweep and gravel road must be made, the stables and offices moved, and a great increase in plantation undertaken. To be sure, all these expenditures would pay for themselves in time - the new fruit-trees would bring a handsome profit in a very few years - it was the most certain thing in the world - but just at present Mr. Elton discovered himself more straitened in a financial way than he had ever expected to be. None could be more surprised at becoming poorly off than the Eltons. Surely single-minded, self-serving behaviour, applied over the steady course of a decade's marriage, ought to have reaped a better reward than this. His caution, and her economy, deserved more.

Mr. Elton knew that he was not to blame, or if he were, it was only in giving way to the fancy of his wife, and being too liberal, too acquiescent, in meeting her wants and plans. In former days, the vicarage had been well enough for a single man, but it was beyond all comparison too squalid for such a family as theirs. Mrs. Elton's assurances that she would never aspire to such a situation as her sister's, nor take the great house at Maple Grove for her model, went for nought; and whenever there was a choice between the two different ways of doing a thing, it was always, "Let us not have anything pitiful. At Maple Grove it was never thought necessary. Let us have *two* orchards - one with cherry trees and the other with apples - I would not quarrel with you for a fortune, my love, over mere money, that would be vulgar - and the six orchards of Maple Grove would be impossible for us to imitate; but I should feel sorry if you did not have all the cherry-pies you liked, Mr. Elton; and you know where there are children, there must be apples."

They were walking out one morning after breakfast, examining their grounds together, and making plans. Mr. Elton readily agreed with his wife.

"Exactly so. You are quite right, my love; you always are. But you do not consider - cherry-trees are six shillings apiece, and they do not come into bearing in the first season you know."

"Oh, but what does that signify? The sooner they *do* come into bearing, the sooner we will have cherries; and we do not care to make ourselves a proverb for shabbiness."

"Certainly not. But I believe we must be satisfied in making no plantings by the sweep this year. Lime-trees, you know, more properly belong to a large estate, like Donwell Abbey, or Hartfield."

"Donwell! I have nothing to say to *that;* I would never try to compare our little land with that great place, or all the pretensions of the Knightleys. You know very well my feelings on that subject. But Hartfield - I think the Vicarage can safely be said to be handsomer, if not larger, than that sad place. It is a great shame to see how Mr. John Knightley has allowed that fine old property to go positively to seed. I do suspect - though it is not above three times I have been to Hartfield since Isabella Knightley was its mistress - that they manage things very poorly there."

"Very true my love. Mr. John Knightley's business takes him too often to London. He is at home but half the time, and cannot be the interested proprietor his brother is, at Donwell. Donwell is a byword for perfection to be sure - I do quite envy Knightley's grounds and his crops, but I never see Hartfield without pity. Those ten children running riot there, little babies and great boys and girls, all shapes and sizes. They can hardly plant three peach trees without them being stripped of fruit at the first chance. A man with ten children cannot be a good gardener."

"To be sure. Nothing is worse than riotous children, I have no patience with them. Mrs. John does not have the way of controlling them, but then it is hard to know where to affix blame: she certainly has not such elegant children as ours. However, I do hope, Mr. E, that when you speak of *envying* Knightley, you mean his gardens only."

"To be sure. What else could I mean?" asked her husband, with a conscious smile.

"Now do not be sly my love; you know very well I mean his wife. I should never wish to bring her name between us, but at times the thought does come into my mind, I confess. I cannot help thinking of what is past."

"My dear Augusta," cried Mr. Elton, too experienced a husband by far not to know when a compliment was called for, and one that is accompanied by pretty sharp criticism of other people, too. "You cannot seriously suppose that I could envy him that domineering, proud wife! You know me better than that, I think. You are a woman who has no equal in Highbury, and no one can be more sensible of the fact than I."

Mrs. Elton smiled complacently, and waited for more, which did not come, as her husband, walking thoughtfully along the new sweep, her arm in his, returned instead to the subject of the plantations.

"But, my dear, about the orchards - I think that two at once may be a difficulty. We had better put in one this summer, and the other next year. It will be wiser."

"Oh, I daresay you are right," said Mrs. Elton, her mind flying away to other matters. "Besides, we might keep the place by the sweep clear in all events, for the statue-garden we will make with the trophies - may I call them? - that we will bring back from the Continent."

"The Continent?" Mr. Elton stopped in his tracks and dropped her arm. "Good heavens, my dear Augusta, I must beg that you will give over thinking of that. Our means having lessened - we must tighten our belts for the next few years at the least. I have spent all my fortune in improvements you know, and much of yours; and it is impossible that we can live in any sort of style on my stipend only. I had hoped that when your uncle died he might leave his fortune to you and your children; it was a very great disappointment that he left everything to Selina."

"Yes, and she needing it not at all! It is too provoking. I cannot understand my uncle. He must have gone positively mad at the end."

"On the contrary, I comprehend his reasoning perfectly; he meant his estate to remain with the elder branch. Do not think I intend a reproach to you, Augusta. But the money would have been a very material consideration. I confess that I did depend upon it for our children; and now, without hope of any inheritance, we are forced upon our own devices - we must absolutely provide for ourselves. I dislike speaking of these matters to you - and you need feel no positive alarm. If we go on as we are, making no further improvements, and spending as little as may be, we will improve our fortunes in another half-dozen years, or perhaps *ten.*"

"So we shall; that's certain. And then it will be time to think about Philip Augustus going to Oxford you know, and the girls' first season; and there will be other things. So really I do agree with you with all my heart, that we must economize, by all manner of means. We must begin almost at once. I assure you that next year we will do that very thing, just as soon as we return from Europe."

It was beginning to rain a little; and as they returned to the house, Mr. Elton endeavoured to make his wife understand, in terms as firm as they were bold, that there could be no Europe, not this year nor the next. "Perhaps when the children are grown up, my love; but if you wanted to go so extremely, we ought not to have built the greenhouse, or set up the barouche-landau. But you must have everything as fine as your sister."

"Oh, sell the carriage then, certainly, sell it," she cried, "if it will make it possible for us to go to Italy. We shall not need *two* carriages, you know, while we are from home; and I cannot bear the strawberry-coloured lining of our barouche, it is of all things the most disgusting. Have you not considered, Mr. E, how very cheap we will live? Why, we can retrench in Italy far better than we can here, where we have a position to maintain. Living is a mere nothing there. Two winters in Italy will make our fortune, I am very sure."

"But the expense of paying a curate," objected Mr. Elton.

"Very true, that's well thought of; but he need not live at the vicarage. Only think, he can take a room in the village - there are some to let at the Crown, and I believe Mrs. Stokes' sister, or some person like that, will take in boarders for a mere nothing. And then we can rent the vicarage to a gentleman's family and turn a pretty penny."

"There is something to that," he said, consideringly. "I don't say there is not."

"But we must fix the orchard plantations first. No gentleman will rent a property that is a positive desert, you know."

"Perhaps not; but I still do not at all understand, my love, why you are so determined to be journeying. It is most uncomfortable, you must be aware, most. You have often heard me speak of my tour to Paris when I finished at the university - and what tedium it was, being such a long while in uncomfortable coaches, and the misery of crossing the water, and the muddy roads, and the unpleasantness of a foreign inn. You cannot conceive of the dirtiness of foreigners. The oily food is what you could not endure. And the children - being among French and Italians and such cattle, cannot be at all good for their health. No, Augusta, I believe we will have to wait until they are older, and we have more money, after all."

Mrs. Elton was not convinced.

The Compleat Mrs Elton

CHAPTER TWO

efore her plans for an Italian tour were at all matured, or indeed, approved by her husband, Mrs. Elton felt a powerful longing to communicate the intelligence of it to Mrs. Knightley. That lady had always irked her by an unspoken assumption of superiority, which was infuriatingly only too well founded; and it was of great satisfaction to Mrs. Elton to have lighted upon something in which she might for once flatter herself as being above Mrs. Knightley, who was no traveller.

Mrs. Elton and the great lady of Donwell Abbey were not on the most cordial of visiting terms. Mrs. Knightley went to considerable lengths to avoid any meeting with the vicar's wife, to whom she felt a very particular aversion; but with both living in the same village, and in the same society, with ties to the church and the regular intercourse of their husbands, complete avoidance was not a possible thing; and when Emma saw Mrs. Elton's donkey-carriage bearing down upon the Donwell gates, she sighed and gave her companion a look of humorous resignation.

"It seems I am fated never to enjoy a quiet tête-à-tête with my dearest friend," she said. "It has been a week at least since I had you quite to myself, my dear Mrs. Weston, and now it is not to be after all."

"We are always so busy with the children," said Mrs. Weston with a smile. Emma had three sons, and Mrs. Weston had two daughters, and in addition to this increase they were at this moment awaiting the reception of another child, not one of their own but a visitor. Mr. Frank Churchill's daughter Jane, a motherless girl who spent much of her time with her father's family, and with her great-aunt, Miss Bates, was expected in Highbury almost any day.

"I did want to hear all about poor little Jane, and I dislike that we must have such a conversation with Mrs. Elton present," Emma complained.

"Never mind, my dear Emma," said Mrs. Weston consolingly. "We must try to recollect that the girl's mother was always a great favourite with Mrs. Elton, and she has a right to be warmly interested in the daughter."

Mrs. Weston was greyer and stouter now, ten years after Emma's marriage; but in spite of several deaths in the family, the latest that of her daughter-in-law, Mrs. Churchill, for whom she was still wearing black ribbons, she was yet a happy woman. It would be hard not to be so, she was sure, with such a husband as Mr. Weston. Though now nearly sixty, he was a hale and robust specimen of that age, and cheery and blithe in his spirits. In such a happy home, with the young affection of their daughters, and frequent visits from their son Frank, who, if a young widower, was also a very wealthy one, Mr. and Mrs. Weston had nothing to wish for, but that Frank should be soon married again.

Mrs. Elton was announced, and after she had seated herself and the state of their own, their husbands, and their respective children's healths were exchanged, her hearers were surprised to find the subject of young Jane Churchill's visit being hurried over. Mrs. Elton only wanted to establish that the girl had not yet come, so that she might hasten to open her darling project to her audience.

"Oh! this Highbury, how tiresome it is, the road is so vilely dusty, my bonnet and sunshade are positively caked. How glad I am that we are likely to be going somewhere soon, that is not so pitiful."

"Why, where are you going, Mrs. Elton?" asked Mrs. Weston civilly, since Emma seemed to be struggling with herself over whether or not to make answer to the contemning of the village.

"To Italy! There's for you, is that not news? Yes, yes, we shall be setting out quite soon, to see Florence, and Rome, and Verona, and such places; and I am sure we shall bring home presents for all our friends. You must place your order with me," she nodded vigorously.

She had her satisfaction; both hearers were duly astonished, and silent for a moment. "I thought Mr. Elton was determined not to go to the Continent - you have persuaded him, then?" Emma ventured.

Mrs. Elton looked as if this supposition was beneath notice. "Oh! That is all but done. He acknowledges that it will do very well for us to remove ourselves from Highbury for a year or two - for the sake of economy, and all that; and it will be the very best thing for the children's educations."

"You do not mean to take the children with you?" asked Mrs. Weston, with concern. "Why, Philip Augustus will be rather a handful in a journey, will he not? and Augusta Phillippa is hardly more than a baby. And then Selina is such a delicate child, too."

"To be sure, that is a consideration. Mr. Perry thinks poor darling Selina may almost be in a decline, her chest is so weak; but the balmy southern climes will be the very cure for her. It will be an education for Philip Augustus in especial - he will grow so very cultured a young man! - and the dear little ones will have their attendants of course, just as they would at home. I can conceive no difficulty at all."

Mr. Weston came in, having walked to Donwell on purpose to fetch his wife, and he quickly caught the tendency of the conversation.

"And is Elton really going!" he cried. "That is news! What a fine thing for you all, to be sure - a change of climate, of scene, of everything. I quite envy you. I was recommending the same for Frank, was not I, Anne, my dear? Every body should go a-travelling, it keeps one young."

"If it does not kill you entirely, with the bad food and water, and dirt, and illnesses," said Emma with alarm. "I confess I have no wish to be travelling myself, and most particularly not with children. There are many dangers that ought to be considered." The older Emma grew, the more she showed that she was her father's daughter; and her disinclination for travel was by now firmly established.

"No, to be sure not; but then you were not brought up to it, as was the case with me," said Mrs. Elton, with a superior smile. "Why, as a girl, I was in constant motion between Bath and Bristol; and it gave me a taste for the sort of thing. What one is accustomed to, one appreciates. But I dare say Mr. Knightley will never desire his family to travel. He is so deeply rooted in this slow old place, after all. Why, you have scarcely been away from Highbury since your marriage. Your wedding tour was to the sea-side, I recollect."

"It was," said Emma, suppressing her indignation, "and we have taken the children there as well, you may also recall. Mr. Knightley is not at all averse to travelling; he thinks nothing of a trip to London, and I have accompanied him, more than once, I assure you, on a jaunt, though I am not at all fond of the city. But to travel abroad with little children - that is what I would never expose myself to. I believe you will find Mr. Perry agrees with me, that it is most unwise."

"But Italy! only think. The music, the statues, the mountains, the orange-groves," said the lady, clasping her hands in affected rapture. "And then travel widens the outlook, you know. I am sure we shall come back to Highbury with entirely new views of the world."

Her listeners displayed so little of the jealousy she hoped to excite, that Mrs. Elton, rather disappointed, took her leave, and drove her donkey-cart into the town, to spread her story to Miss Bates and Mrs. Cole. From them she hoped to receive a full measure of sympathy and envy - indeed, she only feared that Mrs. Cole would herself immediately project a Continental tour, in consequence, that might entirely eclipse the fame and éclat of her own.

Mr. Knightley came in from the farm soon after Mrs. Elton took her leave, and he had the news to hear. His wife and the Westons all spoke at once.

"Italy? - Absurd," was his response. "It is pure folly for Elton to be taking his family there. I expected better sense of him, and I will not believe it until I hear the story from himself. I am surprised that he should allow his wife to entertain such an idea, or suffer her to go about telling people of it."

"It is more likely that she gives the idea to him, I suspect," said Emma slyly.

"Yet, after all, and in some ways, their removing themselves would not be a bad thing," said Mr. Knightley thoughtfully.

"Mr. Knightley! I am surprised. You are generally such a resolute defender of the Eltons - I did not think you would express a wish to get rid of them, so openly."

"You mistake me, Emma. That is not what I mean. Elton is a respectable man and a very good Vicar of Highbury, and I have not an objection to him in the world. He is, perhaps, at fault, upon occasion, in not controlling his wife; but that cannot be the easiest duty in the world, governing either her spending or her tongue."

"Do you mean that the Eltons are in difficulties, Mr. Knightley?" inquired Mrs. Weston.

Her husband had come in while they were talking. "To be sure they are, my dear," he confirmed. "Why, don't you know? Elton has been talking to me and Cole, of that very thing. That greenhouse and the alterations to the Vicarage cost a pretty penny. He has overspent himself, as we all are tempted to do, to be sure, and now must pay the price. He thinks of going abroad to repair."

"How shocking that they cannot live within their income!" said Emma complacently, "and it is all her fault, I am quite convinced. However, I should not think that Italy would be the place for Mrs. Elton to learn economy."

"It is not," Mr. Knightley agreed, "nor shall it be. I have a proposition for our friend Mr. Elton, that I believe will be a much more suitable thing; and while his wife is out of the way making calls, will be the very time to broach it to him."

His hearers all begged to be told what it was.

"Only this. There is a new field for church workers opening in America, and today I have received a letter from a missionary group that is hoping to employ several clergymen. This group is in Boston, but I believe they send ministers out to all the various States and to the territories as well - some to convert the Indians."

"Indians! Only fancy Mrs. Elton among the Red Indians!" breathed Emma, much diverted.

"And with her little children," said Mrs. Weston, distressed. "Surely, Mr. Knightley, that would be most unsafe."

"Elton would most probably be settled in Boston, where he and his family would be as essentially comfortable as in Highbury itself, and live within such means as still remain to him," proceeded Mr. Knightley, thoughtfully, "though to be sure, the farther regions would not do amiss in some ways. The prairies are said to be very healthy for chest complaints."

"And little Selina's chest is weak, I know," murmured Mrs. Weston, "like my little Emily's. The greatest care must be taken of such children."

"The prairies!" said Mr. Weston eagerly. "What an adventure! I wish we could go ourselves, Anne, do not you? Emma, should you not like to venture? To see an Indian or two?"

"Don't talk of it, I beg, Mr. Weston," said his wife with a shudder. "Leave Highbury and go among the Indians, of all outlandish things! I pray you do not mean it."

"Oh, not I, not I. Have no fear. But Elton is a younger man, and a clergyman, like himself, can do much of good in America."

"And Mrs. Elton has always wanted to be going somewhere," said Emma demurely, and not without some suppressed glee. "I think America might be far enough to satisfy even her! But what about her desire for Italy? Can that be done away with?"

"We are being precipitate," said Mr. Knightley, "we do not know that they will go anywhere at all. Now I am aware that they are open to the idea of settling elsewhere for the purpose of retrenchment, however, I shall lay this American project before Elton, and keep on the watch for other prospects that may present themselves. As justice of the peace, and with my brother's law business in London, I hear of various openings, from time to time. Something we must find to help out the good Eltons."

CHAPTER THREE

"America!" exclaimed Mrs. Elton. "Mr. Elton, have you taken leave of your senses? You know we have our trip to Italy in contemplation. How could you think that I would ever consent to go out to a land of savages?"

It was after dinner, the children were asleep, and the Eltons were seated one each side of the fire, looking into their future.

"They are not savages in America, my love. Boston is a very fine city - very handsome - and I am offered a most desirable living, in one of the most important churches. You do not consider how much faster a man of the cloth can get on, in this new country. Why, I should have the importance that, here at home, might scarcely belong to a bishop. In England, you know, it is uncertain what I might make of myself, without influence, connections. In America, my own merit would determine the thing."

"Oh, Mr. Elton, how can you say you have no connections!" his wife protested. "There is my brother Mr. Suckling, and Mr. Knightley would surely do anything for you."

"I have been in Highbury these dozen years, Augusta, and my position is not altered a jot for the better, rather for the worse," he complained. "Your brother has no influence in the Church; and Knightley is not to be depended upon for preferment. Though, to give him his due, it was he who put me in the way of this Boston business."

"I understand. He wishes to be rid of us - or rather, his wife does, and he is ruled by her. I always knew how it would be. But if we are to be exiled, why must it be to

America? Why not Italy, where we can see so many fine paintings? There are no paintings at all in America."

"You are mistaken, my love; there are some very fine ones in Boston, and everything else you like there besides. A high exclusive society - a lady such as yourself might move in the very first ranks, Augusta. Remember they are not used to English people of the best breeding and education: you will be sure to take the city by storm, and rank as a regular Queen of society."

Mrs. Elton was visibly flattered at the prospect, and her husband pressed his advantage.

"It is the New World you know," he continued, "and everything is bigger and better there. We should have a much bigger house, and be able to afford fine gowns for the girls. If we do not choose to return, Philip Augustus shall have the advantage of a Harvard education."

"Oh! How you talk!" said Mrs. Elton, and picked up her sewing with a discontented expression that might have been called a scowl, had it not been upon a lady's face. "As if that were the equal of an Oxford one. No, I beg you will not refer to this matter again, the mere idea distresses me."

If Mr. Elton was prudent enough not to mention the American scheme for some little time, that was not the case with Mrs. Elton's neighbours, who, once the news was spread about, never stopped talking about it at all. The residents of Highbury were not given to travelling, as a rule; and the news that the Eltons were to go abroad on a journey - to Italy or to America did not much signify - created a positive sensation.

Mr. Cole wanted to know if Mr. Elton would convert the Indians, and Mrs. Goddard pleaded with his wife very earnestly to do something about the slave trade. Miss Bates was the most agitated of all, and walked up to the parsonage to talk about it with Mrs. Elton, even though she was growing very stout, and the walk left her puffy and breathless.

"America! Bless me! Only think! What ever would Jane have said? It is at such times as these that I miss her most sadly, Mrs. Elton, as I am sure you do. How she should have enjoyed hearing an account of your plans! It is post time that is the emptiest time of the day to me, you know, for that is when I recollect that I am never to receive a letter from Jane, and never can write to her, either, where she is. But I shall write to dearest Frank. The news may cheer him a little, if anything could: it is barely a twelvemonth since Jane left us, you know, and how I wish that she might have gone with you to the great prairies, which are such a cure for the consumption. Perhaps she might still have been here, had it been thought of."

"We are not going to the prairies," said Mrs. Elton shortly, "if we go to America at all it will be to Boston, which is a very different thing; but I have no idea of it. I am in hopes that Mr. Elton will come to his senses about Italy."

"Boston! Italy! Only think, how you do fly about! Fancy going so far away, quite across the sea! At least, Boston is across the sea. Italy, I do not quite know. There is the Mediterranean, I believe. A very odd place; I never know if it is spelt with two t's, or one, or two r's, or perhaps even *three;* it is so unaccountable. I always say it has a heathenish sound. Not that I have cause to talk of the Mediterranean so very often, but lately, since you have been thinking of going out, I have said the name two or three times, and very strange it sounds. And so it does not make you nervous, to go such a distance from home? I do not believe I ever knew any one who journeyed so far before. To be sure, there is Mrs. Dixon who married and went to Ireland - and Frank took poor Jane to Switzerland - I am so glad that she saw the mountains, while she was still alive. The snow on top of them she said, was very frightful. I am sure I should have been frightened to death, myself, of the snow falling down. Avalanching, I believe, it is called, and very dangerous it is. But little Jane declares that she admires the Alps, of all things. Enscombe, you know, is positively full of the fine engravings they brought back - a great many of them, of different mountains I should say. I never saw so fine a house as Enscombe - we were all so happy there. Everyone so happy."

Miss Bates put her handkerchief to her eyes, and shook her head dolefully. She had made her home at Enscombe in Yorkshire for some years after the death of her old mother; and had nursed her niece devotedly in her sad illness. In gratitude Frank Churchill had settled a sum on her which was sufficient to relieve her from want in her own old age, and now she was returned to her native Highbury where she felt most comfortably at home. The Churchills' little daughter divided her Highbury time between Miss Bates and the Westons, and the next piece of news to be spread through the parlours and drawing-rooms of Highbury, was that of the girl's arrival, which was most joyfully announced by Miss Bates to Mrs. Elton, on the very next day.

"She is with the Westons at this very moment - and will remain for a month or six weeks - sure, she is as happy as possible with their little girls, and Mrs. Weston is so kind - but then her papa has promised she shall make a stay with her Aunt Hetty, too, on condition I do not ply her with too many seed-cakes and good things. He is as careful of her health, after what happened to her poor mother, as even Mr Woodhouse himself could be, poor dear Mr. Woodhouse, who was always such a proverb for carefulness."

"Yes, Mr. Woodhouse is much to be regretted; a fine old gentleman, and always devoted to me, positively," Mrs. Elton replied, with some complacency, "quite an admirer of mine. I remember him very kindly - and it must be these eight years since he went. Yet, on the whole, a good thing for the Knightleys; his death was quite a release for them."

"A good thing! I am quite shocked, Mrs. Elton, how could the loss of dear old Mr. Woodhouse be a good thing?"

"Why, you recollect that the Knightleys were able to get into Donwell Abbey then; and I am sure Knightley could not have wished the removal were even one day later. It was rather too much to be absolutely living at Hartfield with the old gentleman. I felt quite sorry for Knightley, though he took it with the greatest good nature."

"My dear Mrs. Elton! No one could be less likely than Mr. Knightley to entertain such thoughts. I am sure he regretted his dear father-in-law most sincerely."

"Oh, well, I know you are a great favourite with Knightley, Miss Bates," said Mrs. Elton carelessly, "and to be sure, he has done considerable to assist Mr. Elton. It is entirely due to him that this Boston post is offered, and I understand it is splendid, quite splendid. We are quite in Knightley's debt."

This was perhaps more true than Mrs. Elton was aware; for between her husband and Mr. Knightley, some money transactions had been arranged, that had relieved Mr. Elton from certain embarrassments, and which he fully intended to pay back, some day or other.

"Is it so very fine, indeed? That is quite what I should have expected from dear Mr. Knightley. He is generous to a fault. Such good neighbours as we do have in Highbury - even when I was so happy at Enscombe, you know, my heart was always longing after my good friends here."

"I am sure it was," said Mrs. Elton, only half-attending. "I am sure I shall everlastingly be missing you all, when I am at Boston."

And so insensibly, hardly knowing how it happened, Mrs. Elton's talked-about trip to Italy, turned into the absolute fact of emigration to the New World; and almost before she was aware, the arrangements were concluded. A curate was found, inexpensive and hard working, who might be lodged in the village; and a gentleman was to be installed at the vicarage with the view of using it as a shooting-box at certain seasons of the year.

Passage was arranged, clothing and amenities for the journey packed into trunks, and which of the servants were to stay at the vicarage and which to depart, was decided. The Eltons would take out with them a maid-of-all-work and a manservant, and acquire other help according to what their establishment in Boston required. The last of the preparations for their departure on the first of June, was the expected round of calls to take leave; and they were celebrated in so many dinners by their neighbours that in their final fortnight in Highbury they never once dined at home, as every one wanted to hear all the particulars of their great adventure that was to come.

The very last dinner party was given by the Knightleys, and it was a select affair: Mr. and Mrs. John Knightley, Mr. Frank Churchill, Miss Bates, the Coles, and the Westons, were all gathered to do the Eltons honour. Not since her wedding, had such a party been collected especially for her, Mrs. Elton was complacently aware; it would almost have been worth leaving the world she knew, to be so feted, were it not for the disconcerting suspicion that the éclat of the celebration might gain something from the guests' delight in getting rid of her.

However, Mrs. Elton was not capable of containing such an unflattering reflection about herself for very long, and she rejoiced in a very comfortable, preening contemplation of her position in society, which was only to be surpassed by the prominence she would enjoy in Boston.

"I do not expect so *very* much from the place," she told Mrs. Knightley, "I am not so ignorant as to think it is a mere unintellectual landscape, as the modern poet says;

Boston, you know, is the capital of culture in America, quite the capital of culture."

"I hope you shall be extremely comfortable in your new home," said Mrs Knightley civilly, "you will soon be acquainted with all your parishioners, and I am sure you will lack for nothing, in either a social, or a material way."

"Oh! surely not. Boston has the very newest sort of emporiums, I have heard. Every sort of thing that one could possibly want, is to be had there. In fact, I expect a city, like Boston, will be far livelier than an out-of-the-way little place like Highbury. We will dine with so many families, and have such charming concerts, and go to picture-galleries every day - it will be quite a civilized life."

Emma, diverted as well as annoyed by Mrs. Elton's air of importance, tried to catch her husband's eye, but he was calmly occupied in the carving of a majestic saddle of mutton, and did not observe.

"And it is a healthy place?" asked Mrs. Weston anxiously. "I have heard there are swamps in America, where agues and plagues are very rampant."

"Not in Boston, my dear Anne," her husband assured her. "The Eltons will find themselves in a bracing climate, I believe, such as will stimulate health."

"Quite cold in winter. You will freeze, unless you have a very sound brick house with good fires," murmured Mr. John Knightley, with a shudder. He had never been able to conceive how any man with a good house could leave it and cross an ocean for another, but as the Eltons were no particular loss in his estimation, he kept his strictures largely to himself.

"How shocking!" said his wife, "I do hope little Philip Augustus and Selina and Gussie will not be too chilly. The sweet children! You must bring plenty of woollen blankets with you, Mrs. Elton."

"I hope you mean to write to us, Mrs. Elton. We will look forward to your letters, quite anxiously," Mrs. Weston assured her kindly. "You will be our American correspondent."

"Yes, Elton, we will look to you for political intelligence," said Mr. Knightley, passing him a plate of mutton. "You will tell us all about Mr. James Monroe and Mr. John Quincey Adams, and their doings."

"Oh! You will be living in a place with a President," exclaimed Miss Bates. "To think of no longer living in a kingdom. The idea makes me quite dizzy. And our two countries have been so often at war. I wonder if they will again."

"They are not at the present time, Miss Bates, and there is no likelihood of such a thing. The Eltons will be perfectly safe," she was assured on all sides.

"Yes, once they have crossed the sea. That, I confess, is the part that frightens me more than anything. Are you not frightened, Mrs. Elton? You may be ill, you know, upon the sea. Oh! I 'cannot bear to think of it. It is a particularly frightful element."

"Not in the least, a sea voyage is what many ladies have accomplished," Augusta said confidently, "and modern arrangements make all so comfortable. I am sure I shall be a very good sailor. Mine is the very temperament for it. My nerves, my resources, you know, are not like anybody else's. I have a firm resolve, and I am perfectly resolved I shall not be ill. I believe it is only your weak, fainting sort of ladies, who succumb to such vapours."

"Well, you may be very sure that all your old neighbours wish you a safe journey, and Godspeed," said Mr. Knightley good-naturedly.

CHAPTER FOUR

he *Medusa* set sail from Liverpool the second week in June, with Mr. and Mrs. Elton, their three children, and their two servants aboard. Her first sight of the dock was a considerable shock to Mrs. Elton. As the family stood closely together, with their portmanteaux and boxes arrayed about them, she was conscious of a rising sense of discomfort. The Eltons were not being distinguished in any way among the throng, or treated as passengers of pre-eminent importance. People of all sorts and kinds, large families of emigrants, sailors and stewards, visitors and pet animals, dogs, cats, and parrots in cages, caused a scene of bustling confusion that could not fail to bewilder those fresh from a quiet place like Highbury; and the Eltons stood at a loss, without a conductor or any one at all to receive them, or to tell them what to do or where they should be. Mr. Elton saw the expression of dismay upon his wife's face, and made an attempt to cheer her spirits.

"Only look, what a fine ship ours is, my dear. Is it not trim, and stout? Quite a beauty, I declare. Although I ought not to say 'it'; a ship is usually referred to as 'she' you know."

Mrs. Elton shifted her apprehensive gaze from the dock and the people around her, to the ship itself, and her expression did not vary. "It is so small," she protested. "How ever can all these people, and their goods, be carried inside, with safety? I am sure it cannot be safe, Philip."

"Depend upon it, Augusta, the seamen know their business," her husband said with confidence. "It is larger than it looks. Do not be afraid."

"Papa, papa, is that the ship? Shall we sink in it?" asked little Philip Augustus in piercing tones, that raised a shudder in several anxious-appearing persons standing about.

"Hush! hush, my dear, of course we shall not sink, what a thing to say. It is perfectly safe. Only see, the captain over there, with his brass buttons - that is Captain Jennings. He will not let anything happen to us."

"Do you think he is a very safe man?" Mrs. Elton queried nervously.

"Certainly, certainly so. Captain Jennings is as safe as houses. He has a fine reputation. Do you know what a reputation is, little Philip?"

Somehow, with all the confusion and swarms of people, order was in the course of the morning duly brought out of chaos, and passengers and belongings alike were stowed aboard. There was another bad moment when the Eltons perceived that the private, first class cabin they had taken, was a mere bolt hole, scarcely broad enough to fit themselves inside, with the three children in one tiny bunk and Mr. and Mrs. Elton in the other. The servants must fare as best as they might in the common steerage quarters below. To make things worse, a terrible creaking of boards was heard, as the ship moved about in its berth, weighted heavily down by freight and human cargo.

"Will it always be moving about so dreadfully?" asked Mrs. Elton querulously. "If it is no worse, I think - I believe that I shall be a good sailor enough, and not be ill. I do not feel at all ill thus far."

"We are still in port, my love," said Mr. Elton, feeling not unanxious himself, "but we were wise in breakfasting lightly, and I am sure we need anticipate no evil consequences."

"But here is no room for our trunks. How are we to be served, for a voyage of weeks in duration, perhaps, with our goods not to hand, and our servants not near?"

At that moment a sailor with a cheery face and long strings of hair, poked his face into the cabin. "Good afternoon. I am Edward, and you must tell me what you require to make you comfortable. We shall be embarking presently, sir, and tea will then be serving in the saloon. Fresh eggs and pork and greens and baking goods have all been taken aboard, and the feeding will be very fine, you will see. The *Medusa* has better food than almost any other ship I have ever served in."

"And have you served in many, pray?"

"Dear, yes, sir," he said cheerfully, "been at sea since I was not much bigger than your lad here; and this run to Halifax and Boston is a mere nothing."

"You don't think any of us will be - ill?" faltered Mrs. Elton hopefully.

"Why, I couldn't say, to be sure, ma'am, that depends on what good sailors you are. On our last crossing however, hardly a soul was sick. We expect a good fast crossing - storms this time of year have never been heard of - and nowadays there is far more comfort aboard than would have been the case only a few years ago. The *Medusa*, you know, has every convenience. Ladies will hardly know they are at sea at all."

Edward briskly departed to attend to other passengers, and assuring themselves that they were quite equal to making their way about the ship, the Eltons ventured along the passage to the cramped dining quarters, where the novelty of a meal at sea was gone through without any more surprise or displeasure than what the coarseness of the serving implements and the tight fit at table occasioned. The children were delighted at the charming way the plates slid about with every movement of the ship, and the meal was so successfully undergone, that the Eltons congratulated themselves once again upon the excellence of their seamanship. This was premature, however, for by bed-time, they fully perceived that something was amiss with their cabin. The shoes they had taken off, seemed to have slid up onto the walls, and the beds, narrow and thin as they were, appeared to have turned upon their sides.

"Oh, husband, help, help, I am sure this is sinking! We shall all be drowned!" cried Mrs. Elton, and the children awoke and began to wail.

Mr. Elton fumbled about in the darkness, forced open the cabin door and breathed great swallows of the open air. A steward, not Edward, rushed along the passage, and Mr. Elton called out, "I say! Are we all right? Is this a hurricane, or a squall? You don't anticipate our foundering?"

"Just a bit of rain and wind, sir, nothing more" called the man over his shoulder, and ran on. Mr. Elton crawled back into his alarmingly tilting berth and spent the remainder of the long, dark, frightful night trying to soothe his wife and children.

Such nights dawned into days when no one left the tiny, airless cabin, and only listlessly partook a very little of whatever drink or victuals the steward brought; sickness reigned supreme, and Mrs. Elton lay, mercifully oblivious to what her position in the ship's social circles might have been, were she able to struggle to the deck, or into the dark, narrow saloon where such passengers who were not desperately ill, idled away the long daylight hours.

On one particularly smooth and sunny afternoon, Mrs. Elton took a little broth, and then, arraying herself in a large shawl, and with her older children clinging to her skirts and little Augusta Phillipa in her arms, she cautiously undertook the journey to the deck, and there she sat, lost and uncertain, glancing around miserably at her fellow passengers.

"I wish we had gone to Italy," she lamented. "To think that we should be confined to such a dismal little vessel as this, and surrounded by such villains and low people."

"Hush, my dear, you will be overheard. You do not wish to insult any one, whether we are among oddities or no. I think you are feeling better?"

"No, to be sure, not at all. I do not comprehend, Philip, how it is that we are not treated as passengers of the first class. Here we are amongst emigrants, and people who can be of no property at all."

"Why - the sea is a democratising business; and these are young families, going to seek their fortunes in the New World, as we are," her husband tried to assure her, "and we are settled in the best sort of cabin there is upon the ship, after all, Augusta; I made certain of that."

"If you please, ma'am," said a plain, neatly dressed young woman respectfully, "if you are not quite recovered from the sea-unpleasantness, I wonder if it would relieve you to have me hold your baby for a little while? I should be so glad to do so. What a fine one she is."

"Why yes - thank you," said Mrs. Elton, a little less ungraciously. "My maid has been prostrated, like me, but she cannot be expected to have as much spirit as I have, and she is still below. I never have endured any such agony in my life as this crossing. Were I not such a good sailor, I should have suffered dreadfully; only I think the higher the mind, the more resources one has. Are you going out to America as a servant?"

The woman smiled, and explained. "No; my husband is a clergyman, ma'am, and we are going to Boston, intending to undertake missionary work. Our parents are dead, you see, we have no family ties and are alone in the world; and so we thought there would be wide opportunity for good works, in the new world."

"A clergyman! Good heavens. Pray excuse me, madam, for taking you for a servant, but two weeks at sea alters every one's appearance shockingly. Why, Mr. Elton - my caro sposo - is a clergyman too, and is to take up a fine post in charge of the Federal Street Church in Boston. He and Mr. Knightley have been writing to a certain Dr. Channing about his instalment there."

"Are you quite sure, ma'am? Dr. Channing's church is one of the most respected in Boston, and he is a famous man of the cloth. I have never heard that he might be resigning his office."

"Oh! yes, depend upon it, that is what Mr. Elton was told," Mrs. Elton insisted carelessly.

"I do not like to contradict, but my husband, too, has been in correspondence with Dr. Channing; and I know that it is from the Federal Street Church that so many clergymen are sent out, all round the country, to spread the word about man's perfectability, and to talk against the slave trade. I think you will find that Mr. Elton may not be situated at the Federal Street Church, after all, but sent elsewhere, as we expect to be."

"Nonsense! Of course I know what his position will be, better than you can possibly do; he is to be one of the foremost men of the city. An English clergyman, you know, like Mr. Elton, will be quite looked up to by mere Americans. They cannot have the advantages of his education, his cultivation, not even in Federal Street."

Mr. Elton had been listening to this converse with some perturbation. "I beg your pardon, madam - if I may inquire, what is your husband's name?"

An open-faced young man of fresh, healthy appearance moved to his wife's side as she spoke his name, "Mr. Benson."

"Ah, you are Benson? Yes, I believe you were mentioned in one of Dr. Channing's letters, as a young man going to take over one of the new parishes. So, you are making the crossing as the same time as we are, what a very odd thing."

"Yes; God does work in mysterious ways," the young man said cheerfully. "And you are Mr. Elton. Dr. Channing has mentioned you, as well. We are to be brother workers. The good Doctor is quite anti-dogmatical, you know, and likes his clergymen to be doing, rather than speechifying; and I have no doubt that we will be sent to the parishes that stand in greatest need of our practical aid. It is my earnest hope that I may be allowed to do something to help the poor slaves. What a shocking thing slavery is, sir, and such a disgrace to a new nation; we have been blessed in England to be comparatively untouched by the business. Abolition may be slow in coming, but in the meanwhile, there is much good work to be undertaken in helping these poor souls. It is a rich harvest. Perhaps we may be sent out to missions in the South."

"The South? What do you mean, sir? I assure you that I am sorry about slave conditions myself - very sorry - but I was given to understand that I should be working with Dr. Channing himself, directly, and in Boston: not in the South."

"Yes, to be sure you are mistaken," put in Mrs. Elton with energy. "My husband is an established clergyman, very well known in Surrey, in Bath and even in London: you are a young man, just beginning, and may be suited to be sent out to the barbarous Southern regions, but Mr. Elton can look to something better, depend upon it." She nodded vigorously.

Mr. Benson only smiled. "We will see what the good doctor has in mind for us, in due course," he said pleasantly. "For the present, we have the rest of this voyage to perform, in safety I am sure it is to be hoped. Are you feeling strong enough to walk, Maria? We will undoubtedly see much more of you later, Mr. and Mrs. Elton."

Mrs. Benson relinquished Augusta's baby, and with a nod and a courtesy, moved away with her husband.

The Eltons turned to one another with concern. "Philip - what do they mean?" she exclaimed. "It is unthinkable. Sent to the South! I thought you were assured of being in Boston."

"That was my understanding, indeed, my love," he said uncertainly.

CHAPTER FIVE

edraggled and dirty as the Eltons were from four weeks on board the *Medusa,* their spirits were lifted by their first sight of Boston, which was, as its rising fame had heralded, a very handsome city indeed. Fine stone public buildings, of a sufficient antiquity to bespeak extensive and comforting evidence of civilization; and pretty, light-coloured wooden houses ranged up and down green hills, that looked fresh and gay in the open, if intense, sunshine of July.

The travellers were welcomed at the dock by the great man himself, Dr. Channing, a tall, grey-haired man of benignant expression. He would not speak then and there of their prospects, but assured them that such discussions could wait, and in the meanwhile all would be done to make the new arrivals comfortable. They were conducted to be housed in a set of pleasant, good-sized rooms in a rooming house adjacent to the church, kept for visiting clergy and their families.

In a plain but clean room, with bright patchwork quilts upon the bed, and the most modern and convenient of wash-stands, Mrs. Elton was reassured to learn from the landlady that her travel stained garments might be washed and refreshed for very little cost. She had a full minute or two of surprise, however, when she saw that the person sent to wait upon her and her children, was a quiet-spoken young woman of African race. Mrs. Elton stared at the servant for several moments, and at length addressed her with:

"Are you a slave?"

The young woman looked up from the pile of garments she was folding, and smiled. "No, ma'am, though your question is natural enough. I am a free woman; my name is Ella."

"Oh - then please forgive my questions. We are new to America, and know nothing of these things. You were born in slavery, were you?"

"No, ma'am, I was born in Boston. Massachusetts is not a slave state, you know, and any of the coloured people you meet here will be free. Many have formerly been slaves, however, and have escaped in some way or other. My husband was born a slave, and his family is still in the South. We hope to be able to purchase their freedom, some day."

"Well! upon my word, how peculiarly interesting, it is quite a tragedy," exclaimed Mrs. Elton. "Children, do you hear this? This young woman's husband was a slave. There must be something to be done, and if no one will dare to act, then Mr. Elton and myself must. When we are established here, in our own home, Ella, we must see what we can do for yourself and your husband."

The servant thanked her with more quietness than Mrs. Elton's effusion would seem to warrant, and then ventured a question of her own.

"Your husband, then, ma'am, I was given to understand, is one of Dr. Channing's missionaries?"

"Yes - that is, no. I am not yet entirely acquainted with the terms upon which Mr. Elton is to stand; but I believe he is to figure as Dr. Channing's right hand."

"Oh, then, perhaps he will go to the South, and help my people," said the young woman, clasping her hands. "That would be God's work. People there are in such dreadful need, I know your blessed labours will be rewarded."

"Why, I am sure they shall," said Mrs. Elton, rather pleased, "though I do not at all know where we are likely to be stationed, and rather fancy it will be here in Boston."

After a rest and a meal of cold chicken, the travellers began to feel quite restored. Mrs. Elton was seized with a desire to go out walking, to explore the neighbourhood, and her husband made no objection.

"It is quite safe to go promenading," he assured his lady. "In due course, no doubt, we will have a carriage; but it is always best to see a new city on foot, at first, to make intimate acquaintance with all its thoroughfares and byways."

Mrs. Elton hardly listened, being occupied in staring at the different shops that lined the streets. "I declare, Mr. Elton, have you ever seen so many shops? Quite as many as are in Bath, I dare say, and almost as many as in London. Very excellent shops too from the look of them: those ribbands are the latest thing, and that bonnet looks fresh from Paris, I declare."

"It is remarkable, is it not, to see so much ingenuity displayed in the New World," said Mr. Elton. "Far from the fields of manufacture, they have built their own machinery and stores and seem to have quite achieved an independence from our country, in terms of economy as well as politics. I am sure we shall do very well here, Augusta; I do believe it is quite a civilized place, after all."

Mrs. Elton was inclined to agree with him, especially after a walk upon Beacon Hill and a shopping excursion to Market Street, all accomplished within the space of the next two days. The children were enchanted by the variety of goods and toys in the shops, but somewhat disappointed in the people passing in the streets, who looked too much like those back home.

"I thought we would see Indians," said little Philip Augustus in disappointment. "I like seeing the black people, and the Chinamen; but why are there no Indians?"

"Indians are in Indian country," said his father, swinging the boy up onto his shoulder, "and we are not going there."

The Eltons and the Bensons had been to dine with Dr. Channing, but he continued to civilly defer the discussion of where they would live and work, until, as he said, they had accustomed themselves to their new surroundings, and he had made better acquaintance with them and formed a fair impression of his new clergymen's capacities. Not until a week after their arrival, therefore, did the momentous consultation take place. Mrs. Elton waited for her husband in their rooms, anxious to hear tidings of their fate.

"Oh!" she exclaimed to Ella, who was sewing quietly while the children, who had taken a great fancy to her, played at her feet. "I do hope we may remain in this pleasant city. It is so very nice. The lodger next door - what is her name, Mrs. Gilham, says there are so many sweet little literary societies, and musical circles, some of them frequented by the cream of society, and highly educated people from Harvard. But I do not know if it would not be better to go to the South, after all, and help your people, poor things."

"I am sure Dr. Channing will decide what is right," said Ella calmly. "Mr. Elton is such a nice man; he will make a good missionary. English people are always so sympathetic about the poor slaves, and we do admire them for having none in their own country."

At home, Mrs. Elton would never have allowed such open talking from a servant, but she believed she had grasped the idea of American equality, and felt herself able to make more free with Ella than she ever would with her own maid, a Highbury village girl, Kitty, who in truth had not much to say.

Footsteps were heard upon the stairs. "Hark!" said Mrs. Elton, "here he comes, my herald, bearing the news of our fate! Well, my love?" she demanded as he entered, with an indescribable look upon his face. "What is it? Do not hold back the tidings. Break it to me at once!"

"You will find it very surprising," said Mr. Elton, finding his voice after a moment. "I know I am surprised. I hope it will not be too much of a shock to you, and I can do no better than to say it simply. My love - we are to go out to the Indians."

Mrs. Elton fell back in her chair with a shriek.

Ella and Kitty were called upon to administer calming powders and embrocations for the rest of that evening; but Mrs. Elton was no faint spirit, and quickly rallied and recovered her shock. On calmer consideration, she concluded that the only hopeful part of a desperate business was that they were not to depart for six weeks. It would take that long to arrange their outfit and their stores, and for Mr. Elton to learn something about the Indian customs. They were to set out upon the first of September, in hopes of making part of their journey before snow flew. There was a respite, then, time to be spent in Boston during which Mrs. Elton might improve her acquaintance with the place, and enjoy the shopping, the lectures, and the musical concerts to her heart's content. She clung to the thought that, after all, anything might happen - the plans might alter; Dr. Channing might change his mind, or die; or Mr. Elton might leave the church.

In the meanwhile, the Eltons were treated very civilly by Dr. Channing's circle, and they did not at all object to being feted like heroes that were to be. Oyster suppers and chicken dinners, musical parties and dances, were given to them in abundance, all very much as might have proceeded at home, among their friends in Highbury, or in a circle of clergy families in London. The fresh-painted houses were brighter and newer-looking, the hours somewhat earlier and the food more abundant; but the only real novelty in the

Eltons' new American lives was the style of the suppers taken in their own lodging-house, at which all persons in the house, young, old, of high station and low, were expected to sit together round a long table, for the more efficient consumption of tall bowls piled full of cranberry jellies, plates of beefsteaks and fricasseed chickens, heaping mounds of mashed potatoes and turnips, and johnny cakes sweetened with maple-sugar. Despite the excellence and abundance of the food, the high-bred feelings of Mrs. Elton could never become accustomed to meals taken in such common public circumstances, and she invariably took her bread-and-milk in her own bed chamber.

Mrs. Elton had early become fast friends with her lodging-neighbour, Mrs. Gilham, a sociable clergyman's widow, who had some fortune of her own and was pleased to gad about the shops with the English newcomer. It was harder to amalgamate with the earnest young Mrs. Benson, and their intimacy did not at first improve beyond the slight acquaintance they had made aboard ship. Mrs. Elton prided herself on being a woman of activity, and she found the energy and spirits to sally out every day with Mrs. Gilham in search of bonnets and laces; it was not as pleasant to follow the example of Mrs. Benson, who spent long hours in what corresponded to cottage-visiting in England.

The Bensons had been given an assignment as well as the Eltons, and they were to go to work in Maryland. It was arranged that the Eltons would travel together with them some part of the way, before proceeding West. Mrs. Benson, therefore, was particularly interested in learning as much as possible about what would be useful to help the poor people of Maryland; and Mrs. Elton occasionally could not escape being drawn, with an American clergyman's wife, Mrs. Stanley, as guide, on forays in her chariot into the poor quarters of Boston.

"Though," Mrs. Stanley explained, as they rolled along one August day, "there is nothing like such poverty in Boston, as there is in the South. Boston is a rich city, and more to the point a right-thinking one; we would never suffer such slums and poverty as there are in other cities, and as I daresay exists is in your old country."

"Why, there are no slaves at all in England," answered Mrs. Elton, indignantly, "and there were very few poor people at all in Highbury. That is - I think - we gave away soup at the Vicarage to anyone in need; but only very seldom did anyone have to be resigned to the poorhouse. All that sort of thing is exceedingly well arranged for, I would have you know, in England."

"Yes, but Highbury is a prosperous village," put in Mrs. Benson.

"To be sure, I suppose it is," said Mrs. Elton, somewhat surprised; "but how could you know that?"

"Why, I have heard you speak of it a great many times now," said Mrs. Benson, laughing, "of Mr. Knightley, and Mr. Weston, and their wives, and all about conditions in Mr. Elton's parish. Charitable concerns are under the patronage of the good ladies there, and I am sure no one in Highbury ever goes without for very long; but you must know it is a very different thing in England's larger cities and towns."

"Well, to be sure," said Mrs. Elton, "I have seen quite as much of the world as a young woman like yourself can have done, Mrs. Benson; I have spent several seasons in Bath, and I never in my life saw so many beggars there as one sees every day in Boston."

"Bath is a place of fashion," Mrs. Benson reminded her, "yet that city, too, has its poor. Perhaps they are kept rather more out of sight than is the case here. You know the poor are always with us, Mrs. Elton - that fact cannot be escaped. There is positive need of all sorts, everywhere, in

English cities as well as here; starving children, and poor unfortunate girls, and other sights that would break your heart."

"Aye - to be sure," sighed Mrs. Elton, "and I have such a tender heart; I am quite a proverb for it, at home in dear Highbury. But why then did not you and Mr. Benson remain in London, if there is such a field for activity there?"

"I should have been satisfied," was the answer, "but Mr. Benson is more advanced in his ideas. In his correspondence with Dr. Channing, he became imbued with his philosophies, and thought that however urgent are the needs of the poor in London, the condition of the slaves is yet a deeper sort of misery, and he could do the most good in America."

"I don't know if America will thank you for that," exclaimed Mrs. Stanley. "You know we don't like to be taught anything by the old country; and I think you will find slavery a more intractable institution than you give it credit for."

"We have no illusion that we can do anything substantial or immediate toward the abolition," responded Mrs. Benson, "but still, there is much of individual good that can be done for the poor people, and those still enslaved are the most in need of the comforts of the Gospel, to help them to endure."

As proudly as Mrs. Stanley assured her new English friends that Boston was a progressive city where blacks and whites mixed freely, it nevertheless did not escape the notice of either Mrs. Benson or Mrs. Elton that the freeborn blacks did not travel alongside the white citizenry in the public carriages, and that if the shantytown where most of the black population dwelt was not considered a region of misery, then those in other cities must be unspeakable indeed.

The ladies dubiously inspected a series of small wooden shacks by the river, the boards inches apart from one another so as to produce pleasant currents of air in summer, but which would allow snowy blasts to enter in winter. In one room Mrs. Elton counted fourteen abject, ragged human souls, those that were not upon the bare and splintered, dirty floorboards, lying upon a thin mattress together. Their clothing was a moving mass of merest greasy rags, and the odour that emerged was something Mrs. Elton had never encountered before in her life.

"Oh! those poor souls!" she exclaimed, emerging backwards from the black hole of a place, her fingers pinching her long and pointed nose. "How unbearable! How disgusting! How can we ever help them in their wretchedness?"

"We have seen but too many of these places," said Mrs. Benson soberly. "What is being done, Mrs. Stanley?"

"A Ladies' Aid has been formed, and we hope to clear out these slums and have decent lodgings built," that lady said briskly. "These poor people come from up the country, and find no work in town, and have nowhere to turn. It seems an hopeless business, Mrs. Elton; but the American spirit of enterprise will prevail in the end, you may be sure."

"It will be well if it does," said Mrs. Elton faintly, "could not we persuade other ladies to adopt some of those ragged children, and see that they are educated?"

"That would be a good work," agreed Mrs. Benson, "only there are so many children that must be helped. I think, when we reach Maryland, the best thing will be to establish a school, and teach the children decent ways. Sewing, and cooking, in addition to reading and writing, of course; and perhaps we may be able to have some of their parents in night classes. Oh, it will be a fine prospect!"

"I dare say it will," said Mrs. Elton, much subdued, "you have your heart in your work, I see."

"How *can* a human heart turn aside, when one sees those poor children?" cried Mrs. Benson, her eyes flashing.

"All very well and good, but you cannot change the world," said Mrs. Stanley, "to think you can do so is preaching and moonshine. Come, now, and I will take you to inspect a school for young working women - another very deserving and needy class."

By the end of the stay in Boston, Mrs. Elton's head was whirling with the inevitable reaction to all the poverty she had seen and the schemes for its amendment that she had heard proposed. Far from wishing, as in her first days in the city, to spend her time haunting the fancy goods shops, she was now among the most enthusiastic and convinced of converts to charity-work. She was as persuaded as any lady in Boston that this was the highest avocation that could possibly be; and was on fire with new ideas and plans that were to alter the existing abuses and abominations and make a new world in a very short time, an accomplishment for which she would receive due praise and credit.

CHAPTER SIX

The first stage of the Eltons' journey South was taken by stage-coach, which bounced so roughly through the woods and among the stumps, that it took some time for them to learn how to hold on well enough to be able to look out the window. After an interminable day, during which the coach's wheels were several times stuck in mud, they pulled up at an inn, which was, Mrs. Elton was to discover, a very typical specimen of what might be found in American travels in general. The passengers alighted, their bones aching from their uncomfortable ordeal, and were ushered into a room where a long, boarding-house table was covered with pork, salt fish, potatoes and bread, while flies buzzed over all. Several strangers had already begun heartily feeding, looking neither to the right nor the left of them. Mrs. Elton at once disdained to join this company, and ordered that her food be served in her own room.

The landlord, an unwholesome-looking man with long, greasy grey hair and many missing teeth, looked up briefly from the head of the table, where he sat with his face in a bowl of bread-and-milk. "Oh, no you don't, old woman," he addressed her. Mrs. Elton looked about, to see who he could possibly be addressing so rudely.

"Yes, you, the English party. My old woman can't be doing for everybody different; you're no better'n anybody else, and if you want to eat, must sup with the common herd."

Mrs. Elton tossed her head, and refused to deign a reply. "You may do as you like, Mr. Elton, about this most offensive insult; but the children and I will endure no more.

Will you show us to our rooms, please," she haughtily addressed the man's wife, a blowsy woman some years younger than her husband, who was placing dishes upon the table.

"I can't now, dearie, I'm serving, but if you want to go to your room, it's up the stairs, take a left turning. I'll bring you something later," she hissed in a loud whisper, turning her head from her husband, who heard what she said.

"If you do that, old woman, it's out of your own uncommon softness; I wouldn't put up with the airs and graces of that English old woman however. But it's on your own head, be it," he said indifferently.

Some time later, Mrs. Elton and her little maid Kitty had given the children some sort of wash, when the inn keeper's wife appeared with a tray holding a bowl of bread-and-milk that looked as if it might have been the identical bowl left over from the landlord's dinner. "Here you are. I do understand, you keeping to your old country ways," she said, not unkindly, "but you'll see, if you don't mind me saying so, it won't answer here. America, you know, is a free country, and everybody's equal; we don't put up with anybody that gives themselves airs and graces and makes out they're better nor anybody else. Some folks might take offence at that, see. So, a word to the wise; and if you'll come down and take breakfast with everybody else, it'll spare me many an angry word from my husband."

Mrs. Elton was so taken aback by this extraordinary speech, that she made no answer, and only stared, leaving Mr. Elton to thank the landlady, and Kitty to feed the children helpings of bread and milk.

The next morning the travellers resumed the coach, and half the day was not sufficient for Mrs. Elton to vent her feelings.

"I never heard the like! Impertinent, half-bred, presuming creatures, without the least idea how to address a lady! And dirty! Did you see the flies - and the linen last night, I could barely close my eyes, for fear of vermin. Boston was pretty well, Mr. Elton, but I misdoubt that in the rest of the country accommodations will be of the order of the barn and the pig stye. God knows what it shall be tonight. Not that I suppose it is possible to fare worse than we have thus far."

"Never mind, Mrs. Elton," said Mrs. Benson kindly, "we will reach New York in a few days, and that city, they say, is quite as fine as Boston. We may pass some time there comfortably before we venture south."

"Yes; I should wish to visit some of the churches in New York," said her husband. "But I fear, Mrs. Elton, if you find the inns in the North-East part of the country lacking, you will not at all like what we may discover farther South, where conditions are generally considered to be far poorer, I believe."

"But in farming communities - the wide open fields - surely we will find the inns cleaner and the food fresher in such places," she protested, with a shudder.

"Now, see here," spoke up a strange man with a broad, red face who was crowded in to make the eighth in the coach, and whom Mrs. Elton suspected of having had too much to drink, though it still wanted hours before noon, "I'm getting tired of hearing you abuse our fine country and its ways, missus. Why, everybody knows that America is the finest country in the world, and its inns and hotels have the latest comforts, and the best victuals anywhere. Your crowned heads and tyrants of Europe could live no better than we do upon the road, I calculate, old woman."

Mrs. Elton was irritated enough to reply, "And how do you know that? Have you ever travelled in Europe, sir?"

"No; but I have no need to do any so foolish a thing. There ain't no reason, when everyone knows America can't be beat. Every freeborn man in America can tell you it is our government as makes us free, while you are lorded over by lords, and are no better than slaves. Why, good lack, no one can have the motive to run a decent business, or treat customers right, when it's all for the sake of they lords."

"Slaves! It is your country that keeps slaves, I believe," said Mrs. Elton, with a sniff.

"There is something in what you say," cried Mr. Elton hastily, "exactly so. But, my dear sir, no country is perfect; and you will admit that the inn in which we passed last night, was no model."

"Why, no, I don't say it is the very best; I have travelled a great deal, being a merchant, you know - Winthrop by name, and I sell all manner of dry goods in my emporium in Worcester - and I come down to New York two and three times a year - but yet it is a comfortable place enough. Good food, good cheer, you know; and everyone treated as equals; what more could you ask? I reckon your English old woman will have to change some of her snobbish idees, if she wants to get along with we."

Mrs. Elton tossed her head, and did not deign to answer.

Some miles farther on, the coach stopped for another couple, and despite the protests of the already seated passengers, that the coach was intended for eight and no more, a man and his wife must be made room for. "We're bound to give them room," insisted the coachman, "and you can shove your fripperies aside, I reckon; this lady's got only her bandbox, and them children can sit on their ma's lap."

"But we have paid in advance for our seats," protested Mr. Elton.

"Can't be helped; these folks is paying customers, too, and I won't leave 'em in the dust."

The merchant was the only one who seemed entirely glad to welcome the new inhabitants of the coach, on the grounds that they were "more Americans." He quickly found out that the new man had a thriving farm tools business, and for the next hours the only sound that was heard above the jolting noise of the coach, was that of their conversation, which grew louder, as the merchant shared the contents of his little brown bottle with his new friend, and they grew increasingly moved to assert their opinions of all things English. The woman drew herself back into her bonnet, and from what Mrs. Elton could see of her face, looked grim and unsocial, while the menfolk made free.

"That's what riles me up about them English. Take these folks here. Think they're better than what we are, and never do a lick of work," Mr. Winthrop concluded a long oration, with a satisfied air.

"Sir," said Mrs. Elton, unable to stifle her indignity, "do you know that you are speaking of the cloth - these two gentlemen are clergymen!"

"Oh, are they? Well, meant no offence, to be sure, against the reverends - but I calculate as how it's true enough of English people 'in gineral.' I've met enough of 'em to know."

"Yes; it's remarkable how little English folks know of how things work in a real, thriving, bustling commercial-minded place like our great nation," chimed in his new friend, a beady-eyed little man named Carter.

With that, the two men willingly enough left the subject of the English, and returned to their hymn to business conditions. "Wheat'll go sky high this fall, I guess," commented the farm dealer.

"Yes, and that always affects everything. I don't quite reckon what goods I shall buy in New York, depends on what the market will be. Perhaps your business is not so affected by fluctuations?"

"No, that's right enough; people always has to farm."

"I declare that's so. Sound, practical activity, in business and farming - that's what this country is run upon. Not such aristocratical nonsense as they have in the old country."

And so on.

The journey was tedious, and all parties were relieved to reach the rising city of New York. The Eltons were enchanted by its beauty, the wide harbour and the green islands scattered in it; and then Manhattan itself, with its broad avenues, great shops, and handsome dwellings on the lower portion of the island, surrounding the Battery, is too well known to require any description. The rest of the island, as the passengers saw from their carriage, contained several charming villages such as that of Bloomingdale, and stretches of rolling farmland. Even before she had alighted from the coach, Mrs. Elton was ready to praise what she had seen of the city. "One might almost be in London itself," she cried, "though indeed it is not London, and there are no doubt many differences, this does have the appearance of a place where it might be possible to live a refined existence."

There was every reason to think so; for Dr. Channing had provided both the Eltons and the Bensons with introductions to persons of some consequence in the town, and a very pleasant fortnight was spent in visiting their handsome homes, where silk-covered furniture, carpeted floors, European china and silver, were on display, and the beautifully laid tables and excellently cooked, carved and served foods, helped put the boarding-house experiences quite out of Mrs. Elton's head. Yet it was still America, for every man seemed to think it his civic duty to spit in the streets; and at one of the city's greatest theatres, the visitors were shocked by the manners of the theatre-goers, which were far more rough and uncultivated, with men in their open shirts putting their feet up on the seats before them, and more spitting and talking and drinking going on during the performance, than they had ever witnessed in London.

Going to church was a considerable contrast, for in New York, the Eltons observed with some surprise, the churchgoers were almost exclusively ladies, daintily dressed in the height of the fashion. The men were somewhere else - anywhere else, in the parks, or at the races, smoking or strolling - but wherever they were, they evidently did not feel themselves called upon to spend any part of their Sundays inside a church. Mr. Elton and Mr. Benson had a good deal of worried talk about this, but concluded that there was little they could do to attack this universal custom, as they were not to be stationed at New York; no doubt, upon the whole, Mr. Benson would find still more serious abuses in the South, and Mr. Elton among the Indians.

Art galleries, shops of all varieties, schools and institutes for the poor, and Dorcas societies for the ladies, were visited in this whirling fortnight, but what Mrs. Elton enjoyed most, and used to speak of reminiscently in later days, was the strolling pageant of Broadway. This was a street of almost unprecedented broadness and length, more than thirty blocks long, where ladies promenaded dressed in the French fashion, their elaborate silks, pelisses and parasols a-flutter with satin ribbons. Families drove out for an airing in handsome carriages, but these were forced to share the streets with the pigs and dogs that dined upon the refuse every householder threw into the midst of the handsome, broad avenue.

In the evenings, the best shops, restaurants and theatres were lighted up with the new gaslight, and Mrs. Elton was delighted to see that every good private house seemed to have its own block of ice, quite as in the fashionable regions of London, making the most elegant entertainment possible; so that the butter on the dinner-tables was not mere loose grease, but formed into pretty patties, set in moulds, and decorated with green ferns.

Especially popular were great public establishments such as the oyster-palaces, where quantities of the fresh molluscs were swallowed, by clusters of men and women and children reaching out for them as fast as they could be handed over. The range of amusements possible in New York was positively dazzling; and most diverting of all was the street-dancing performed by troupes of black dancers, a form of entertainment that was entirely new to the visitors, who were bewitched by the performers' gaiety and liveliness. Some of the free blacks in New York, evidently persons of some means, were as elegantly attired as any of the white ladies of fashion, and all joined together in the promenade on Broadway, with perfect amity. It was true that, as always, there were neighbourhoods where the most sordid poverty prevailed; and the two ministerial couples examined many such regions during their sojourn, as was their duty. Despite these sobering glimpses, upon the whole the impressions of New York that they took away were of swirling excitement. They were sorry to depart, and long remembered what they had seen.

Two ferries and two coaches were necessary to bring the party as far as Philadelphia; in the boats, the male passengers amused themselves by chewing tobacco and spitting liberally all over the deck, and Mrs. Elton spent the entire journey holding her skirts and her children away from the expectorations, with an indescribably pained expression.

Their visit here was a short one, only long enough for them to discern that Philadelphia was another fine city, rapidly building, although decidedly less refined than Boston, and less lively than New York. In the evenings, the city was entirely dark; there were none of the modern gas-lamps that prevailed elsewhere, and all was as shut and as silent as midnight at Highbury, which the visitors thought surprising, considering the city's substantial size. As they were in Philadelphia over Sunday, services were attended at the principal Episcopalian church of the place; the party was given a kind welcome by the clergyman, Rev. Harding and his family, with whom they stayed for several days, and were introduced into their social circle. From these encounters, Mrs. Elton concluded that religion was given a far more prominent place in the lives of the Philadelphians than at New York, or than was the case at home, where worship every Sunday, and attention to the needs of their parishioners, still did not take up so much time and thought as even unclerical ladies seemed to spend on their churchly concerns in this American city.

Services were long, and although Rev. Harding was a genial man, kind and thoughtful in his own family circle, Mrs. Elton could not admire his ponderous sermon, and secretly contrasted it to her husband's sensible, well-spoken ones; nor did she care for the way that silence and sobriety were strictly enforced by law all day long on Sunday. Even the streets had chains slung across them to discourage carriage driving, and there were none of the parties and gaieties such as the Eltons had enjoyed in other places.

Their hostess Mrs. Harding was a precise, tidily dressed person, in her steel-grey satin and lace cap, who ruled her plain but handsome household and her numerous daughters with kindly severity. Her house was one of solid comfort, if not luxury, with well-trained and well-treated, free black servants, so that she was left with little to do in the way of domestic work; but the ordering of the household, and of her daughters, and her church work, occupied her time very fully. Mrs. Elton and Mrs. Benson joined Mrs. Harding at the meeting of her sewing-circle, where a dozen ladies diligently sewed garments for the poor, and listened to readings about the foreign missions.

Despite her real, if somewhat officious, wish to do good, and to support her husband's missionary endeavours, Mrs. Elton felt that the praiseworthy activity of this large ministerial household was more confined and less varied even than life in such a quiet little place as her own home village. After the second evening, in which she saw that husbands and wives were always kept quite separate, and the conversation seemed limited to not very acute, rote criticisms of the second preacher's afternoon sermon, Mrs. Elton felt an imperative desire to speak.

"Do you not have any other form of evening entertainment?" she inquired somewhat abruptly. "The theatre, or card parties? Dances, balls?"

Before she finished speaking, Mrs. Harding and her sister, Miss Fuller, exchanged pained glances.

"Mrs. Elton, you are new to our great country," said her hostess in a tone of patient politeness, "and do not perhaps realize that things that are done in old England, may not quite conform with what are accepted customs here. The theatre, and cards, and things of that sort, *we* consider to be really not quite nice; certainly not acceptable in a clergyman's family."

"And for my part," put in Miss Fuller, "I vastly prefer a quiet evening sewing, and having improving talk with my sister, and my nieces. It is so much nicer, and more proper, than listening to the worldly talk of gentlemen, which we could not be expected to understand, and is hardly fit for our ears."

"Do they have many balls in England, in the place you come from?" asked a young Miss Harding in tentative tones.

Mrs. Elton brightened. "To be sure we do. There are very grand balls in society, in London; but even in our little village, there are dances that occur quite *impromptu*, every fortnight or so, with twelve or fourteen couple. Even though growing quite an old married woman, I still do enjoy a turn, I own."

"You actually - dance, yourself?" asked Mrs. Harding, clearly shocked. "You don't mean it?"

"Why, yes, certainly, from time to time, I do; we do not consider it so wicked as you seem to do."

"Rapidly moving bodies can only lead to one thing," pronounced the dame firmly, and turned the subject to a mission to New Zealand that was then outfitting.

Mrs. Elton was not particularly sorry to leave Philadelphia, and her impressions of Washington were not something to make a figure in history. The English travellers were impressed by the Capitol, which they esteemed a most beautiful building, handsomely set among plantings, high up so as to command a wonderful view; and they thought the city itself well designed, on a vast and regular scheme, certain to be most impressive when completed. While visiting the seat of government, Mr. Elton made several forays to the office of the Bureau of Indian Affairs, in order to learn what he could about the people amongst whom he was soon to be working. What he told his wife made her spirit rise with indignation.

"They are always talking of their liberty, these Americans," she complained, as they were readying for the night in their Washington boarding-house, "and of how they will be tyrannized over by no king; yet not only do they permit slavery themselves, but they treat the Indian people no better than dogs."

"I believe you are right, my love; but it will be wisest not to say so before any American gentlemen, it will not quite do. They believe, you know, in Manifest Destiny and Eminent Domain, and suchlike doctrines, and so do many people in England; so you had best not mention it."

"I hope I know better than to make a scene, Mr. Elton, no lady ever would; but what do you mean by saying that we believe in Manifest Destiny in England - is that not a name invented by Mr. Monroe, and is it not just another way of saying that the white man should take everything? I am very glad that Mr. John Quincy Adams should be President now, instead; perhaps he will have more gentlemanlike ideas."

"Come to bed, Augusta. It is not like you to be trying to puzzle out matters that are men's business; you know it is wrong and unbecoming for women to think of public affairs, and I can only suppose you are tempted to it owing to these travels of ours - for in general, it is better for women to remain at home, and to take their ideas from their menfolk."

"Now you are sounding quite like an American, indeed," said his wife resentfully, "that is how they talk; and you know it was never *my* wish to come here, though I have followed my lord and master, as is my duty. However, I cannot help but see what is before my eyes; and that I do see the things that are wrong in this country, you cannot attempt to deny."

"Of course much of what you say is right in principle; it is a great shame to take land from the Indians, and slavery is an abomination wherever it is to be found; but surely, my dear, you can see that, in the end, the white man *must* have everything: you would not have the dark races on top? They are hardly capable of governing themselves."

"How can they know until they are tried," began Mrs. Elton, heatedly, but her husband only said, "Hush, hush," and blew out the candle.

.

CHAPTER SEVEN

*I*t was in Baltimore that Mrs. Elton was first waited upon by a slave. This first experience was in no way remarkable or singular in nature; it consisted of nothing more than her knowledge that the two women waiting at table at their inn on their first night in the city were not freedwomen, but slaves. This was sufficient. Both Mrs. Elton and Mrs. Benson felt a rising sensation of horror as they watched the quiet movements of these two young women, who were placing the platters of herring and corn bread before the party. Unlike the movements of every person they had heretofore seen in their lives, the movements of these girls were not being undertaken of their own free will. An entire picture-gallery of the system of slavery, complete with captives, beatings, cruelties unimagined, families torn apart, and everything else they had ever heard and read about with sorrow and pity, filled their minds, and both women found it difficult to swallow their food.

That night, when one of the slave women showed the party to their rooms, and bustled about fetching water and performing little tasks, Mrs. Elton, who had learned something already in her travels to America, forbore to inquire about her condition, or to ask her what it felt like to be enslaved. She only watched, and saw that this particular serving-woman did not seem to be in any observable way less cared for, or unhealthy, or noticeably unhappier than the free black servants she had seen in the North; and she pondered this, and knew not what to think.

Mr. Elton was made uncomfortable by discussions about slavery, but his wife knew that the subject was very close to Mrs. Benson's heart, and the next morning, when they were sitting alone after breakfast, she asked for her views, now that she was in a slave territory.

"I do not exactly know. That is what we are here to learn, and to alleviate in some small manner, if we may," she said earnestly. "I have been told that here in Baltimore, slavery is not found in its very worst form; some of the slaves have no worse a life, outwardly, than ordinary working men and women, but yet it *is* slavery, and they, and we, can never forget it."

"It is painful, unspeakably shocking, for any English person to contemplate this sad condition," returned Mrs. Elton with emphasis, "and I do not see how the good people of America can stand for it."

The two women sat in the hotel courtyard, Mrs. Elton's children playing about them, and watched the squadron of slaves attached to the inn, busily performing their various tasks. The young women, scarves twined about their heads, worked in laundry room and kitchen; the men, in their neat quilted jackets, did odd jobs about the house and yard. All were occupied, but when addressed, the visitors noticed that their manners were superior, and less sullen and rude than Mrs. Elton had frequently found in white servants in the Northern boarding-houses.

"We cannot form an accurate impression on our first day," said Mrs. Benson thoughtfully, "but the condition of the slaves shall be the study of mine and my husband's lives, and we are to begin tomorrow: Mr. Benson has arranged for us to visit one of the large farms, or plantations, where we will see for ourselves how things are done there. You will like to come?"

"To be sure I shall. We are not to set out for the West immediately, and I should like to see as much as I can of a slave state, first. Mr. Elton cannot very well object, as you are going."

On the morrow, therefore, the Eltons and the Bensons were driven to a farm, where for the first time they saw slave quarters, the deplorable dark cabins and huts where the slaves slept; as marked a contrast as could be imagined to the planter's own handsome house. The planter, Mr. Foster, was quite amiable and willing to speak to the party, and explain to them his methods of farming, and ways of dealing with his slaves. "I am not a slave purchaser," he hastened to assure the visitors, "I inherited my workers from my father, who was a very good man; and it is our tradition that all our people are most humanely treated."

"Are you acquainted with any places where this is not particularly the case?" asked Mrs. Elton.

Visibly surprised to be so boldly addressed by a lady, the planter hesitated a moment before replying. "No - that is, you understand, all *our* neighbours are enlightened gentlefolk. No unreasonable whippings, or anything of that sort, goes on; this is a most genteel neighbourhood."

"But you do whip your slaves?"

"Why, only when they won't heed anything else, for they must be kept in order some way, you know; but our slaves are so well-behaved, that it is hardly ever necessary. Only if one should try to run away, or get drunk, or drive a waggon too fast, or act insolent, or misbehave outrageously."

"And then you beat them - with what?"

"Why, *I* do not beat them, do not think that for a moment. We employ a person to do the necessary. There was a fellow we thought stole a visitor's silver pen - it turned out later it was no such thing - but it was needful to make an example, to prevent other such incidents. He received fifteen lashes, which is not very many. However, I can assure you that such things hardly ever do occur, so it is not worth talking of. And let me say, madam, that it does concern me, and even hurts me, that this indelicate subject is the very one visitors from the North perpetually inquire about, when it is a matter that they can never be expected to understand, not being slaveowners themselves."

The women had already been confounded into silence, and it was Mr. Benson who asked about families being separated, and children "sold South."

"Such abuses never occur here, sir, I assure you. We do not sell slaves; as I intimated, we consider our people as family. Only truly incorrigible cases - old Lycidas, a regularly bad drunkard; and Esther - it is not quite delicate to speak of her, before ladies, but she occasioned endless trouble among the men - eighteen children she had, all told, before we sent her off, and sold the children. To good homes, mind, not any low dealers; and very likely workers they all made. You can comprehend that to rid the place of a few trouble-makers, is to the benefit of the good workers."

"I think," said Mr. Benson soberly, as the carriage drove the clerical party back into the city, "we have our work cut out for us, Ella."

"Yes," she replied. "It is very sure that we will be sowing the seed in tears."

"I have never been so thankful that we are not to remain in the South," said Mrs. Elton, with a shudder. "There is a great work to be done here, but I have not the courage or the heart for it. Mrs. Benson, I used to fancy myself a heroine, who would do wonders, in removing abuses; but these three months acquaintance have taught me that you are the heroine, not I. You and Mr. Benson are fit for great tasks. I do not feel myself equal to them."

"Yes - it is very painful," agreed her husband, shaking his head. "We cannot be glad enough that there is not such an evil institution in England as slavery; and hope that it can be removed from this country in the natural operations of time, so that America may one day be as fair and untainted a land as ours. Benson, we leave you to your appointed work, and go on for the West tomorrow. That is where our duty calls. I have letters from Dr. Channing, telling me of the fine church that is being established in St. Louis, and in whose vineyards we may toil. Augusta," he turned to his wife, "on our venture West, we may be forced to do without many amenities that we have been accustomed to in the larger cities; but you are agreed that we shall proceed on our appointed way, and not remain in the South?"

"With all my heart," she said fervently.

The Compleat Mrs Elton

CHAPTER EIGHT

The Eltons did not arrive in St. Louis until nearly the end of the October of 1825, after enduring travails along the way such as they never could have envisioned in all their comfortable lives back home in England. They journeyed by coach as far as Kentucky, but from that point on, they were forced to proceed in no better than a rough-hewn, ox-drawn wagon, and with only themselves to depend upon; for the maid Kitty had balked at going out to the "Red Indians" and begged to remain in Baltimore with the kind Bensons. Sam, the young groom who had come out to be their man of all work, decided that all the work he might do for the Eltons would not benefit himself as much as taking a claim on land of his own, and in consequence he had taken his savings and made off to become a smallholder in Kentucky.

Ten miles a day on a wagon track that was often no more than a rocky rut; meals that consisted of a paste made of cornmeal; the hitherto unknown sensation of being always dirty, always hungry: the children crying miserably, and no doctor, no safe Mr. Perry to give tonics and embrocations for cough and fever. The Eltons no longer resembled the sleek and civilized pair who had left Highbury, what seemed like positive ages ago. No one in that town would have recognized the skinny scarecrow, his grim wife and dirty children as the once proud Elton family. Nevertheless, when they at last reached St. Louis, their future headquarters, where they were to winter, they were alive, healthy, and in hopeful spirits.

It was a rapidly growing, frontier city of six thousand souls that they found, centred around a rising Cathedral, the wonder of the west. Steamboats plied the river, the muddy streets ran with livestock, and fur traders and riverboat men mingled in the numerous saloons. The Eltons were thankful that they retained a supply of greenbacks, what remained of their savings, and funds provided for them for the journey by Dr. Channing; this made it possible for them to take rooms at the Missouri Hotel on the muddy streets of Main and Morgan, a two-story log structure whose sign depicted the image of a buffalo. Once, Mrs. Elton would have scorned this building as too heathenish and rough even to enter; now it appeared a pinnacle of civilization, and she thankfully led her children inside.

It was one of the happiest moments of her life, to be brought a large wooden tub full of hot water for washing; and to see the children, clean, bathed and tucked into a real featherbed was fairly joy unbounded. The supper table too: ham, beans, yams and berry pie were a finer feast than the Eltons had enjoyed for many weeks, and the only pity was that in their half-starved condition they could not do justice to it.

There was no doubt that St. Louis, the bustling "Gateway City," was an improvement over life on the trail. The large central square with its wooden pavilion and stalls teeming with men busily trading furs and food supplies, was reassuringly civilized. It might be observed that the beaver seemed to be a great feature of St. Louis life; it was the main fur brought in for trade, and the inhabitants were all outfitted in beaver coats, beaver trousers, beaver hats and beaver boots. "It is all so terribly rough," said Mrs. Elton with a sigh, "but it does look prospering."

"I am sure we shall do well here," replied Mr. Elton, enthusiastically. "There is the cathedral: do you see? Quite an impressive building! Remarkable that such a structure can be hewn in the wilderness. It speaks well for American enterprise. This is my given destination, Augusta, and so, if you will remain at the hotel with the children, where I can be secure of your safety, I will present my letters of introduction there."

Mrs. Elton was not sorry to have an afternoon's rest, and to obtain some mid-day victuals for herself and the children, but it was near dinner time when her husband at last returned.

"Well? What news? Are we to remain here, Mr. Elton?" she inquired anxiously.

"Papa, I saw a buffalo head! And ever so many Indians!" cried young Philip Augustus.

"Did you find us a nice little house, Papa?" Selina wanted to know.

"Not so many questions, my dear ones," said Mr. Elton wearily, "it has been a long day, and not entirely successful."

"Not successful! Why on earth should that be, Mr. Elton? Tell me what can be the matter? Surely in that handsome cathedral, there is work for a clergyman?" asked Mrs. Elton, alarmed.

"Yes, Augusta, there is, but we have made a little miscalculation."

"Miscalculation?" What do you mean? To do with the cathedral? But it is a famous place. We have been hearing about it forever; it is spoken of as the great religious centre of the West, to be. Is it not so?"

Mrs. Elton sat down upon the bed, and anxiously awaited her husband's answer.

"It is a veritable cathedral, in truth, Augusta - but - it is a Catholic one."

"Catholic?"

"Yes. I have been to see the Bishop - a very kind man, Bishop Rosati. An Italian. The cathedral was undertaken and built by Bishop DeBourg, and finished last year; and they have all kinds of fine works in progress. That is so far true enough. A seminary for the Indians - a model school, with everything being taught - even an orchestra and a choir, for their musical education - yes, these enterprises will indeed be the envy and admiration of the West! But in the end, it is a Catholic institution, Augusta, and I am not a Catholic."

Mrs. Elton stared. "Can you not work with them? Surely the same good works can be undertaken by Catholic and Anglican ministers?"

"No; they will not have me. They are as kind as possible, and will give us help, and guidance, to be sure. We are to receive an introduction to some Presbyterian clergymen who have established a missionary settlement outside the city, to Anglicise the Indians."

"But that is the work you are to do, is it not? Surely you can join them? Where is this settlement?"

"It is near the Great Osage Village, upriver. They are missionaries, and preach to the Indians to save their souls; their wives teach them the Bible, as well as reading and writing and useful arts like spinning and weaving. Bishop Rosati believes they are getting on very well. No; more to our purpose is that an Episcopalian Church, corresponding closely with our ministry, has been established by a banker of the town. The clergyman there is called Horrell; but you see it is only a small church. I am to see him tomorrow, and perhaps he will have some advice."

The Eltons went to bed feeling very low, but this mood did not last out the following day. Mr. Horrell was the man they wanted. A sensible-spoken, educated man, though dressed in the inevitable beaver costume, he explained that he had received letters from Dr. Channing, and was delighted to see Mr. Elton, a man of education and ability, who had already proved his and his family's capacity for endurance by the journey they had undertaken to the Far West.

"You are seasoned pioneers now," Mr. Horrell assured Mr. Elton, "and are just what is needed." He and his two young curates could handle the demands of their town parish, but there was good work to be done among the Indians, and the Eltons would serve admirably. The banker, Mr. Riddick, and fellow merchant parishioners, considered that taking the Gospel to the Indians was the best way to tame them, and render them harmless to deal with by turning them into peaceful souls instead of marauding savages who hampered commerce throughout the West. A circle of businessmen would raise funds for a mission led by Mr. Elton. He and his family would be provided with supplies enough to make the river journey up the Missouri by keelboat, to the frontier where they would set forth on their appointed mission: nothing less than to educate the wild Comanche Indians.

This was not exactly the hopeful prospect Mrs. Elton had figured to herself, but it was the best chance that offered. To be sure, they might remain in St. Louis, but without a clergy berth for Mr. Elton, he must turn shopkeeper or trapper; and Mrs. Elton quite agreed that it was better that he retain his calling, even if it meant they must travel to the far ends of the earth to obtain an aboriginal parish. This adventure, however, need not be faced for some months yet, for all agreed it would be folly to "step West" in the autumn; the days were mild, but snow would soon fly, and the Eltons did not need much persuading to agree to spend the winter in safety and comfort in St. Louis, before venturing down the Missouri to the wild Indian country.

The Compleat Mrs Elton

CHAPTER NINE

*I*n the April of 1827, the keelboat *Flora* left Ft. Osage, the last white settlement of any size on the Missouri. The Eltons had been kindly met at Harmony Village, where the two Presbyterian ministers and their wives had everything in train for teaching the cooperative and friendly Arikawa Indians, who already could speak English, and were relatively prosperous owing to a thriving activity in going back and forth to St. Louis to trade their pelts. "These are not like the Indians you will find upriver," the Rev. McAllister, an earnest, red-haired young man, warned Mr. Elton. "The Arikawa - the Omaha - the Blackfeet - are not inordinately dangerous, but we hear very bad things of the Comanche, and if the Indian Removal Bill is passed, there may be open war."

"In Washington I remember there was talk of removing the Cherokee, Delaware and Kickapoo to the southern plains," replied Mr. Elton, "and Senator Benton, with whom I was privileged to have some conversation in St. Louis, is making great progress in the land session treaties. The Indians will surely be removed from Missouri territory in the space of a very few years. However, I have heard of no such plans relating to the Comanche. Nobody seems to have had much contact with them."

"They are masters of the art of not being found," agreed Rev. McAllister, "but depend upon it, when a white man intrudes into their territory, they will appear. I am not at ease about you making this journey with your family - the Comanche are scalpers, you know, and the danger from them is very great."

"Of course, I would not take my family into the wilderness without protection," Mr. Elton assured him, "but there is quite a large party to accompany us as far as Ft. Montgomery, where the garrison will protect us. We shall be quite safe."

"And travel on a keelboat? - for a lady like Mrs. Elton, and her young children?" put in Mrs. McAllister anxiously. Her own hands were hardened with incessant work, and she knew at a glance that Mrs. Elton, whose English finery was still fairly in evidence, lacked experience of life in the wilds.

Mr. Elton smiled. "You do not know my wife," he said, "nothing daunts her. She is equal to anything; and she is very glad to have found the little Indian maiden to help her."

For an orphaned young girl of the Harmony community, Little Bear, had declared herself willing to travel with the English missionary family, and to care for their children; and Mrs. Elton had thankfully engaged her. The girl was well taught, and could talk about the story of Jonah and the Whale by the hour together, for it had impressed her very much; and more importantly she was able to instruct her mistress in many things that would be needful to know in a wild country. The children were fond of Little Bear, and Mrs. Elton took comfort in the knowledge that she would have the company of another woman aboard the keelboat; for there was no other.

The *Flora* was a fine stout barge, sixty feet long, with thirty souls aboard: the captain and his crew including helmsmen, fireman and carpenter, cook, and sailors, accounted for one third, but there were also French fur traders and American hunters, intent on establishing trading posts upriver. Not all those aboard were traders; a man from Boston, who called himself an ethnologist, was making a study of the different Indians to be encountered, and there

were two young Englishmen, who described themselves
cheerfully as 'remittance men'.

"Second sons, both of us," explained Mr. Whitney,
"wanting to make our fortunes in the West." It was pleasing
to the Eltons hear the home accents again, and both Mr.
Whitney and Mr. Pierce enjoyed playing with the children,
and made many polite attentions to the comfort of their
mother, which she much appreciated, for conditions aboard
the keelboat were crude in the extreme. The growing pile of
furs, collected by the hunters on their days ashore, were
stored in the centre of the boat, and smelled hideously.
There was a grate for cooking on deck, and the kitchen
performances, with game hung all about, often produced as
high an odour as the furs. Many cords of wood had to be
burned daily, to keep the paddle wheels turning, but at times
when there was little wind, the crewmen were obliged to pole
the boat forward. They wore few clothes, and took no care
of their language, when about their work, and Mrs. Elton felt
obliged to keep herself confined in the close, smelly cabin
with its one crude porthole. The children enjoyed sliding on
the piles of furs, when they were let to do so; but the heat, in
the May sunshine, was considerable, and Mrs. Elton used to
lie for hour after hour in her bunk, feeling that she was past
speech, past everything. Whenever she ventured out upon
the deck, there were sure to be males behaving coarsely:
spitting, performing private functions, using vile language,
singing, drinking, quarrelling.

After a week of enduring such misery, Mrs. Elton
could bear to keep to the cabin no longer, and she and the
children began to spend more time out on the deck. They
were becoming accustomed to the sights and sounds of the
men; and there was comfort in knowing that, even if most of
them could not, strictly speaking, be called gentlemen, they
bore her no ill will, would not deliberately harm her, and

would in fact fight to defend her if needful. From the time she attained to this sensible reflection, Mrs. Elton was more comfortable, and the men's attitude toward her became more natural as well.

Daily, parties went ashore, and at such times anything might happen. The keelboat pushed over to the banks, and dropped anchor; a number of the men went ashore to collect firewood, or to trade in the Indian villages along the river. Mr. and Mrs. Elton ventured into many such villages, and the children were much entertained at seeing braves wearing leggings trimmed with skunk, and shoes embroidered with porcupine quills. They learned a little of the sign language, though many signs had to do with fighting and war and these Mrs. Elton did not care for the children to learn. Thus far, it had never occurred to her children that Indians could be dangerous, and she wanted to keep them from this knowledge for as long as possible.

To little Philip Augustus and his sisters, Indians were people who wore clothing crafted from animal skins, far superior to their own dirty dresses and shirts that looked so poor now they were torn and shabby. An Indian might care for his skins by rubbing earth and water in them, and they only looked the better and were the softer. The Indians they met liked the children, and would give them corn bread baked in corn husks, and boiled beans, which tasted better than the weevily cakes cooked aboard the boat. Their tipis were cool and comfortable, shed water in rainy weather and were cosy with furs in cool. Boys often went naked, and Philip Augustus envied them; they had their own horses too, and they slept on buffalo robes.

"Why can't we live like the Indians, Mamma?" asked Philip Augustus, when Mrs. Elton insisted on their washing vigorously after a visit to a village. "They don't have to wash."

"That's just like a boy," said Selina disdainfully, "always wanting to be dirty. We are ladies and not Indians."

"That's right, my own. A lady is a lady anywhere, and we must remain civilized, wherever we are," said Mrs. Elton.

"I don't want to be civilized, I want to shoot a bow and arrow," complained her son.

"So you shall, when you are a man," she agreed.

"Now, now, Augusta, do not coddle him. A boy in these Western lands must learn such skills. He shall take lessons from Trapper Jean, a very good shot; he shoots with the Indians every winter up in Canada, and has brought down a grizzly eleven feet tall, he tells me."

"Will I be able to do that?" asked Philip Augustus, pleased.

"Perhaps; one day."

At the end of June the keelboat's progress was stopped by low water, and some trade goods were off loaded, to lighten it. A party of Mandan Indians approached the boat offering delicacies such as buffalo tongues in exchange for any goods the traders did not want, such as whiskey; but whiskey was carefully hoarded and the Indians had to be contented with small metal tools and utensils instead. Some of these men, the Eltons noted, had their faces marked with smallpox, but they did not seem ill, and were helpful in showing the hunting parties where rabbits and ducks were most plentiful. Mr. Elton joined a fishing party, and was proud of making an enormous catch, a catfish that must have weighed nearly fifty pounds, which he brought in with only a little help from a brave called Fishcatcher: this fed the whole boat as well as numerous visiting Indians for a two-day feast.

With the lightened boat, movement was again possible, and in another week a large Sioux village was reached, where the inhabitants lived in leather tipis, and ate their dogs. They were also remarkable for their beautifully decorated buckskin clothing, in which, they helpfully told the ethnographer, they also wrapped their dead, who they stowed them in trees. Mr. Prescott was very taken with these details, which he communicated to the two young Englishmen and the Eltons, but Mrs. Elton only sighed, "It does seem as if the Indians are more barbaric the farther West we go."

The hunting was improving. The hunters now came back to the boat with elk, pronghorn and antelope, and all fared sumptuously. Mr. Elton's status as a gentleman and a clergyman, which bore little significance on the river, paled beside the fact that by the end of summer, he was acclaimed and recognized not only as a good fisherman but a fair shot. Mrs. Elton was not sure - but she was in a way to think that her husband was quite enjoying himself.

One evening, as they sat over their venison and berries, she accused him of caring more for the wild West than for Highbury.

"Why, the two are hardly to be compared, Augusta," he answered mildly. "They are so widely different. But this American life is more stirring than I expected, I confess. Such fine, free country; excellent scenery, and the hunting is magnificent: exactly so."

"I like America more than England," said Philip Augustus, decidedly.

"I do too," agreed little Gussie. "In England we did not hear such stories as Little Bear tells us, about witch-spirits, and the great shaman, and the wolf that ate the world."

"No, there was only Miss Edgeworth and the moral tales," said Selina, making a face. "Do you remember how Miss Bates used to scold us for shouting like Indians?"

"And how Mrs. Knightley said Phillie was a wild child for breaking the window with his ball."

"And going to church - we had to sit so still, but they gave us sweetcake afterwards. And on Christmas, oh, the sugared fruit - do you remember, Gussie, and the oranges?"

"No, I don't, Phillie," she answered, injured. "I never ate an orange."

"You did. Oh, sister, you are forgetting about home!"

"We were clean there all the time, and me and Selina slept in a featherbed with Kitty, I know that," said little Gussie.

"No, that was at Boston. Don't you remember? It was cold, and there were no wild horses, like here, but we had much better things to eat - roast beef, and apple dumplings."

"Mamma, can't Little Bear bake us an apple dumpling?"

"You know she cannot," said Mrs. Elton, with a sigh, "there is only corn flour, and open fires. Oh, I wish - "

Mr. Elton stopped her with a look. "Never mind, Augusta," he said cheerfully, "a great land will be built here, and we shall all have dumplings and roasted hams, every Sunday."

"That's not what Indians eat," said Philip Augustus, "but Trapper Jean says the Army's going to chase all the Indians out of Free Indian land, and then we can have it all. Do you think that is fair, Papa?"

"My boy, we won't speak of this now. It will be many a day before the Indians are gone from Indian territory. They go where the buffalo goes, you know."

Ft. Montgomery was as far as the keelboat would travel; the store of trading goods was spent, and autumn was setting in. The Eltons and some of the hunters were to spend the winter inside the wooden fort, and in the warm September and October days much hunting was done, and stores of meat and berries were collected and smoked, to build a supply of eatables, against the snows. The boat returned downriver, laden with furs, and carrying those traders who were bringing them back to St. Louis for sale. It promised to be a comfortable winter, and come spring, Mr. Elton and his family would settle in an Indian village, where his missionary efforts could begin in earnest.

CHAPTER TEN

*M*r. Elton spent the winter making plans for his work with the Indians; Blackfeet, Mandan and Comanche had villages in this part of eastern Kansas, and he was certain of having much influence, and converting many souls. With those Blackfeet and Mandan who approached the fort in twos and threes, hoping for a trade, or a meal, Mr. Elton did indeed make some impression. They were willing enough to listen to his stories about the white man's god for hours, by a warm fire in the fort, and it mattered not that they did not understand one word in forty. "Great Talk-Man," they called him, and even those whites who remained, the garrison soldiers, some French traders, and the Englishmen, liked to listen, as other forms of entertainment were few enough.

It was a peaceful time. Supplies held out, and sickness did not attack the little settlement. Mrs. Elton learnt to fashion clothing out of buckskin and beaver, and she spent half of each morning instructing her daughters, while Philip Augustus followed the French traders about, listening to their stories about hunting.

"I told you the children would learn French," said Mr. Elton triumphantly, but Mrs. Elton only shook her head. "With what an accent!"

It was in April, when the ground was still wet with melting snow, that the Comanches came.

The settlers in the fort could hear them from a long way off, the drumming sound of many horses thundering, and white-faced they made their preparations, dividing up the arms. French Pierre, climbing up to the lookout-hole, cried out, the note of terror clear in his voice. "Here they come. Mon Dieu! There are hundreds of them!"

There was nothing to be done. The defense of the fort did not last half an hour. The soldiers stationed themselves in the yard to shoot at the Indians as they circled the fort; a few of the riders fell, but the yard was quickly filled with a whirlwind of murderous activity. Hundreds of Comanche, armed with fourteen-foot lances, bows and arrows, stormed the fort, and they were more than a match for men whose clumsy rifles had to be continually reloaded, when there was no time to reload. It was a scene of confusion and unimaginable gore, as men were clubbed, speared, scalped, and in moments, piles of settlers and soldiers alike lay dead. Mrs. Elton was struck by a hard blow on the head that stunned her, and she was barely aware of being pulled somewhere by the hair, little Gussie yanked from her arms.

"You woman, you watch!" a Comanche brave intoned in her dazed ear, holding her head, and with horror that she could hardly comprehend, she witnessed the sight of her husband being scalped before her eyes. "Good God - save yourself, Augusta, and the children," was the last cry she heard. Young Philip Augustus launched himself toward his father and was swept aside with a blow. Mrs. Elton was pulled up behind a brave on a horse, and was carried away as the fort burned behind her; then she fell unconscious, and knew no more.

When she awoke she was in a tipi, and her clothes had been stripped from her body; she was wrapped in skins. Her head hurt brutally and throbbed to the horrible rhythm of the wild singing and tomtoms outside. She managed to half sit up, and saw that her son lay nearby, still unconscious, and Selina was there too, cowering under a blanket. Mrs.

Elton weakly held out her hands and the child crept toward her.

"Father," she whispered.

"Yes - I know."

They cried silently together. At last Mrs. Elton sat up. "It all happened so fast, Selina! Only think. He could not have felt much, or for long; it was over in an instant."

"Do you truly think so?"

"Yes, it was mercifully quick. We must never think of it. We must be strong. But Gussie, Gussie too! She is not here? You have not seen her?"

Selina shook her head, tears in her eyes, and the two were quiet.

Philip Augustus moaned, and rolled over. Mrs. Elton looked about the tipi and found a waterskin, patted some water on his face, then held it to his lips. They clung together for how long they never knew, listening to the warlike sound of drums outside, until someone parted the opening of the tipi, and entered. The three on the floor stiffened in fright. It was a Comanche woman, carrying a pan of cornbread, which she slapped down before them, then retreated. Mrs. Elton and her son and daughter ate ravenously, then, from sheer exhaustion and grief, they slept.

When they woke the sun was streaming in, and the Indian woman entered again and motioned for them to get up and come outside. They were led before a broad, muscled and tall Comanche warrior in buckskin, his face elaborately tattooed, his ears pierced, his hair greased and tied with brushes made of porcupine quills. His scalp was painted with clay, and ornamented with buffalo horns.

"Ee-wunee-keem," he grunted.

The Indian woman said to Mrs. Elton, "He say come here."

"No," she said firmly.

The woman took a plaited thong and wrapped it about her arms, so hard it hurt. She jerked the thong, and Mrs. Elton fell to her knees in the dirt. She stood up with difficulty.

By gestures, the warrior gave her to understand that she was to be his woman. She spat on the ground. Seeing a piece of bone lying in the dust, she stooped, and even though her two arms were bound together, she lifted the bone and flung it in the warrior's face. It rebounded against his nose, harmlessly, and he stared at her in surprise. The woman made a startled noise and backed away.

The warrior made a contemptuous gesture and said something in the Comanche tongue, and turned away.

The woman told her, with some relish, "He say you devil woman. Not be his wife, too much trouble. You work for me, be my slave."

Mrs. Elton looked unconcerned. "Very well. I shall help with your work. That is fair. What must we do first?"

"You and girl - plenty to do. What I say. Sewing, cooking, taking down the tents, putting up. Make moccasins - grind corn - you see. But the boy, he cannot stay with you. Must live with the braves."

There did not seem any objection to make, so Mrs. Elton nodded once, and followed the woman back to the tipi.

All that long summer, Mrs. Elton and Selina worked harder than they ever would have believed it was possible to work. They were treated as slaves, sometimes kicked and shouted at, but no further attempts were made to force Mrs. Elton to be a warrior's wife. Some of the younger braves looked at young Selina speculatively, but Mrs. Elton kept her close by her side at all times.

The braves also watched Philip Augustus closely, to see if he showed signs of wanting to avenge his father's death; but the lad was of a peaceable disposition, and inclined to accept the situation as it was. He soon made friends among other boys his age, and by the end of the summer had slid into their ways and teachings.

The Comanche were, above all things, great horsemen. Their herd was vast, for they were highly skilled at lassoing wild horses with strips of buffalo hide, and they kept hundreds of the animals at their different water holes. Each brave owned many horses, and they spent much of their time practising, so that every man could perform the most daring tricks: dropping his body down the side of his horse while charging, dangling by the heel while full armed with bow and lance.

The women supported their men by doing all the work in camp. Mrs. Elton saw little of her son, and only from a distance; he looked as much like an Indian as any of the boys, and was always on a horse. They might have lived in different worlds. Mrs. Elton was the lowest of the women, and did whatever anyone else wanted her to do; she spent many hours performing the worst work of the camp, scraping smelly buffalo skins with a bone scraper, then pressing a paste of animal offal, grease and water into the skins and pulling and stretching them for days on end, to tan them. She helped in the making of clothes - the buckskin breechclouts, the deerskin leggings, and bear robes, until she thought she never in her life would get the smell of dead animal skins out of her nostrils. It was the women, too, who tore down the camp whenever the tribe or some part of the tribe moved, as happened frequently; and then the tipis had to be set up all over again in the new location. Mrs. Elton got so she could put up a heavy buffalo-skin tipi herself in a quarter of an hour.

Grey Owl, the old woman who gave her most of her orders, made her life as miserable as possible, with many kicks and barked-out words. One morning, when Mrs. Elton had been scraping skins for five hours, with nothing to eat, Grey Owl refused to give her food, and struck her a blow across the shoulders with a club, for daring to ask. It was bad enough that she was hungry, but little Selina sat beside her, thin and crying silently from hunger too, and suddenly Mrs. Elton would bear no more. She rose up, grabbed the club, and beat the woman to the ground. For the rest of the day she sat shaking, and every time an Indian approached she feared being beaten or killed; but oddly, there seemed to be more respect for her after this. Oriah, the brave who had wanted to take her for his wife, and was one of the highest-ranking men in the tribe, made a point of walking past her tipi and said, "Humph, you Warrior Squaw," in a manner faintly approving.

That was her name, Warrior Squaw; and from this time things grew easier for Mrs. Elton and Selina. They were now treated as equals with the other women, and as their skills improved - Selina was quite an adept at weaving with porcupine-quills - they were accepted still more fully and given less onerous work to do. Mrs. Elton did not know it but part of the reason for their rise in status was owing to Philip Augustus's skill with bow and arrow; he was considered one of the ablest young men, and had been initiated into manhood and given the name Bright Feather.

It was during Mrs. Elton's third summer with the Indians that a party of white men rode boldly into the Comanche village. This showed considerable courage, but there were only three riders, so they could present little threat, and they were not molested. The braves Oriah and Horned Owl, and Chief Silver Buffalo, indicated that they would receive the visitors formally. Women were excluded from the council, of course, but the talking went on for many hours, and Mrs. Elton helped in the preparations for a banquet, which included dishes such as pemmican, berries and nuts pounded and roasted in intestines, and a complicated tripe dish.

She was curious as to who the white men were and what they could want, but she had no idea that their visit had anything to do with herself, until a brave came to summon her from her tent. She and Selina followed him to the fire. She glanced first at the rows of young braves seated behind the chiefs in their most formal regalia, and was surprised to see that Bright Feather was not seated in his usual place among the youths, but in an unprecedented spot for so young a man, directly beside the chief himself.

Mrs. Elton now looked carefully at the visitors. They were like any white men found so far west, dark brown in colour from head to foot, from the caked-in dirt, and dressed in buckskins like any man, white or Indian. Two were French trappers, and Mrs. Elton suddenly started: she knew them! They were French Jean and French Pierre, who had been on the keelboat with the Eltons three years ago. The third man was older, and bald, and was looking at her penetratingly, as if he could not believe what he was seeing.

Then Mrs. Elton knew. It was her husband! Philip - not dead at all! Rapidly she remembered that she had been told that people did not always die from scalping: but what on earth - She could have screamed with the shock and joy, but three years among the Indians had given her a training in how to behave as a squaw that did not falter, even though Selina, by her side, gripped her hand as hard as she could.

"Approach, Warrior Squaw and her chicken."

As Mrs. Elton numbly obeyed, it flashed through her mind to wonder just how she and Selina must appear to Mr. Elton. They wore long, one-piece dresses of buckskin and moccasins on their feet; their hair fell down their backs and was held with leather thongs. Selina had grown tall, and they were both deeply tanned; Mrs. Elton's muscles had hardened, and she knew her appearance must be as altered, and she as difficult to recognize, as he was.

"Warrior Squaw, this visitor tells us you are his woman. Is it true?"

She spoke up clearly. "It is true. He is my husband, and Bright Feather and Little Chicken are his children."

"Warrior Squaw, we have no quarrel with these people. We will treat them as honoured guests. We acknowledge your husband, and you may take him to your tent."

Mrs. Elton did not know how she reached her husband's side, nor how they walked to the tipi together, but as soon as they were inside they clasped each other in a close embrace, and laughed and cried. She was the first to recover.

"Oh, my caro sposo, how can you be alive? I saw - we saw - " and her voice trembled.

"Yes, I was knocked down and hit hard on the head, and then, scalped," he said, his voice trembling. "I was left for dead, but I did not die; and the trappers, who were away from the fort at the time of the massacre, returned and found me. I had lost a great deal of blood, but they kindly nursed me back to health, and I have lived and travelled with them all this time. But Augusta - we did not know where you were taken. Have you been - are you - ?"

He could say no more. "No," she said proudly, "Oriah tried to take me as his wife, but I refused, and Selina and I have not been harmed."

"Thank God," he breathed, "thank God. You do not know the fears I have endured, for you all. But you are well - and Philip Augustus too - a veritable young Indian, he appears!"

They laughed a little together. Then Augusta said softly, "Our Gussie, you know, was killed in the massacre."

"I know," he replied, "there was nothing French Pierre or Jean could do for her. So many died."

"And you have lived with them - ?"

"I have been searching for you all this time, Augusta. Pierre and Jean move around a great deal, in their trapping, and I have been helping them; I could do no less, you know, they have been so good. And everywhere we have gone we have looked for the Comanche - but the tribe is so scattered, so fast moving."

"Yes, we are known as Centaurs of the Prairie," said Augusta proudly.

"We!" he said, amused, and continued, "The different groups of Comanche can only be approached with caution, for it is never known which are on the warpath, or what will set them off. The government is attempting to remove them, you know, and they are determined to fight back; that is why they attacked the fort that day, in revenge for these removals. There are thousands of Comanche - it was always uncertain that we ever could find your encampment."

"I did not know."

"It has been a weary search; we have been in Kansas and Texas, and were moving north, as the trappers are returning to Montreal. Your tribe is very far north for Comanche - we never expected to find any here. This is Dakota country; did you know?"

"They do not tell the squaws much," she returned dryly.

"Augusta, do you suppose - will they permit you to leave with me? Otherwise we must return with soldiers, but we would wish to avoid this if possible."

"I think they will. We have served them well, done much work these three years. Can we - Philip, do you think there is any way in which we might hope to return together to civilized country?"

"I do not even know where that is," he said bitterly, "and I have nothing to help us get there; I am still without a great deal of strength. The best we can hope for, I think, is to accompany the Frenchmen north, and make our way back to civilized lands in the course of time."

"Oh, if only we can!" she said fervently.

CHAPTER ELEVEN

*M*r. and Mrs. Elton placed their request before the elders of the Comanche tribe, and after a day and a night of deliberations, their wish was granted: Warrior Squaw had served the tribe well, and might have her freedom. As her lawful husband was arrived, it was agreed that the Great Spirit meant it should be so. Her daughter might go with her, but Bright Feather - after all the training he had been given, and the promise he showed of becoming a great brave, the Comanche were inclined to keep him. However, they acknowledged his duty to his own White Father, and assured him it would be his own free choice.

The young man himself was divided in his feelings. "Might not I remain for some time longer?" he asked his father. "Of course I want to be with you and Mamma, but I am Comanche, now, too. And Great Silver Buffalo has said - he says that I might become a great chief myself, one day. Already only Antelope Boy and Swift Arrow can shoot an antelope at greater distance, and there are ever so many more riding tricks for me to learn - I know there are."

"My boy," said Mr. Elton gently, "it is once for all. If you remain with the Indians, you will in all probability never see your parents or your real country again. You may feel that you belong with the Comanches; but the fact is that their future is dark and uncertain. The Americans will persevere in the clearances - they must prevail in the end, it is impossible that it should be otherwise. The Comanche will be killed off, those that survive the epidemics, which are already making great depredations among all the tribes."

"Then I ought to stay and help them," the boy said stoutly.

"If you feel that you owe them your loyalty. But you owe your own people loyalty too, and remember that these Comanche are the same that killed your little sister."

"And scalped your father," Mrs. Elton put in dryly.

"It was because the Americans would kill them - that was the reason."

"That is true enough. You must decide; you are only fifteen, Philip Augustus, but you have proved yourself a man, and I would not wish to make it a matter of obedience. There is another thing to consider, as well. We have a long and arduous journey ahead of us, travelling east with the trappers. Your family may need you, to help us return to the civilized places where your mother, and sister, and I, truly do belong."

"Yes," the boy said slowly, "if you need me, I will come with you. Please do not think - of course I shall, if you wish it. But, Papa, you came out into these wild countries yourself, to convert the Indians. Are you to give up your mission? "

"Yes, Philip, that is my intention. I have seen enough of the Far West, to take a very different view than what I had before. The Indians, for all the harm the Comanche warriors did us, have their own lives and beliefs; I have lived in Indian country long enough to respect them for what they are. They deserve better than to be displaced by the Americans, or forced to take on our religion, if it comes to that."

"I am glad you think so, Papa," said the boy earnestly.

"And are we really to go home, Papa?" asked Selina wistfully.

"That is part of the reason I wish to reach Canada. It is an English colony: we will be on home ground."

"Yes!" exclaimed Mrs. Elton. "God grant that we may reach it. And Bright Feather - Philip Augustus?"

The boy looked at his mother and sister and lifted his chin. "I will come with you, Papa."

To help ensure that the parting would be peaceable, the French traders and Mr. Elton presented Chief Great White Buffalo with such little presents as remained to them from their stores - some beads, mirrors, and knives. These were only tokens, but the chief received them graciously, in the spirit in which they were offered, and granted the Eltons permission to take the horses that had been made over to the use of Mrs. Elton and the children during their sojourn in the Comanche Nation. The Comanche were rich in horses, if nothing else, having hundreds in camp, both wild and tamed, and acquired who knows how; for they were highly proficient horse thieves, and considered that nobody minded about a few horses more or less.

The journey was unremarkable, and made easier for the Eltons and the trappers by virtue of their now being equally accustomed to travel in the bush. Well mounted, with a goodly supply of pemmican, cornmeal and shot, the party endured no discomforts they were not long hardened to; Philip Augustus proved his worth by showing himself a finer shot than even the trappers, and they ate well on elk and bear. They encountered few Indians, and no white men, on their journey east, as they made their way through the Wisconsin wilderness, wound around the Minnesota lakes, and crossed into Canada in the autumn of 1831.

The winter was spent in the new settlement called Tawa Town, on the site of the former village of the Ottawa Indians, who had been removed to a reservation at Blanchard's Fork. Little enough was there when they arrived, only a lodge and a few cabins, the Row Tavern, and a French trading post fitted out with a light to show the location of a certain sharp bend in the river. The most noticeable physical feature of the area was the Black Swamp; but the pioneers had been busily draining it, and the newcomers were told all about a man named Johnny Appleseed who had passed through and left a fine stand of growing apple trees. With so much enterprise going on about them, the Eltons themselves were not idle. The pelts that Philip Augustus had accumulated were as rich a store as Pierre and Jean had together, and with some of this capital the Eltons opened a store, taking over the dry goods of a shopkeeper who was consumptive, and had been recommended the more southerly prairie country for his cure.

If, in Highbury, Mrs. Elton could never have dreamt of a storekeeper being entertained at her own dinner table, still less could she ever have conceived that she might one day keep a store herself. Yet in Tawa Town it was another thing, and to her own and her family's surprise, she proved exceedingly adept at the work. It occurred to her that "Eltons" need not sell only dry goods, but might aspire to be an emporium like those she had read about in Chicago. Accordingly, she used some of the profits in building a handsome, two-storied, commercial log palace, and stocked it with goods of all sorts, that she ordered sent from the city: warm shirts and mufflers, boots and farm implements, lengths of dress goods, baby linen and furniture. It was, she proudly said, to be the first Department Store in Canada, and sure to make their fortune in a very few years.

This Department Store turned out to be principally Mrs. Elton's own concern. Mr. Elton was nominally the President, and kept to his office, working on accounts and orders, and providing an air of masculine authority; but it was Mrs. Elton who dealt with the public, ordered the goods, and was the ruling body. She was supremely happy in this work, and, in her activity, gave little thought to the defects of Tawa

Town's society; but in spite of the store's rising success, by the second year of its establishment she could see that residence in Tawa Town would not do for a permanency. In the local academy, where the children had their classes, the teaching was only that of a backwoods graded school: this was not the finishing education Selina ought to have had, far less was it tending toward the Harvard or Oxford education of a gentleman, for Philip Augustus.

Then Mr. Elton was unhappy. He drooped, and was disconsolate; and Mrs. Elton could see how at loose ends a man was, when not in his proper profession. If his views had changed, and he no longer felt the call to Evangelise the Indians, he still believed it was more his calling to be a minister than a storekeeper, an English gentleman than an Canadian merchant; and he began to talk more frequently of home.

In their comfortable, three-roomed log cabin, Mrs. Elton was no longer served by Little Bear, for that maiden had remained behind with the Comanche, and married a brave. The family's help was all from the old country now, but this did not mean superior serving. After a long day in the store, Mrs. Elton now was faced with the prospect of a slatternly girl, Sally, to serve up the hot dinner of ham, beans and maple syrup, with plenty of what North Americans called 'sass'. Mrs. Elton looked forward to a useful conversation at the dinner table about stocks for the spring, but it was not to be.

"I see in the Lady's Book just arrived that bonnets are poke-shaped now. We must get some in," she declared energetically, "and men's jackets are shorter. There is no excuse for Tawa Town not to be fashionable, and I am determined it shall be the equal of larger places, ere long. Who says Canadians are out of knowledge of the wider world?"

Sally came in holding the ham by its bone, and thumped it down before Mr. Elton to be carved.

"Pray, do not hold the bone like that Sally - and Mr. Elton will use the silver knife, not the kitchen knife..."

"Well! I don't need to be talked to like that, Miz, I hope you recollect I am a lady the equal of yourself!"

"A lady!"

"Yes, I will have you know; I am only working to save up for a dress, so I won't have to go about in only my petticoat no longer; you won't think me your inferior, when I am married to Jacob Horner!"

"Sally, surely we need not discuss either your dress or your social standing at dinner. Did you do a baking of bread, as I required? I see none on the table."

"No - this here boy of yours told me off to clean his boots and there wasn't no time; I calculate you can eat hard tack, same as everybody else, for all you think you're fine quality. Well, I won't have any more of such face, and I'll be off."

She flounced out of the room, and Mrs. Elton looked at her husband in despair.

"That is the fourth girl in a year. We really have no luck with these Canadian servants."

"Well, Mamma, if you won't let them sit at the table with us, they believe you are putting on airs," Selina explained patiently.

"Even after all our time in America, the Far West, and now Upper Canada, with all we have experienced, I never *can* endure servants sitting at the table," murmured Mrs. Elton. "It seems to me that these Canadian servants are even worse and more insolent than the American ones."

"That is because they have emigrated from England, where they were in service, and used to being treated as inferiors," Mr. Elton reminded her, "and they want to show that it is a different matter, now they have come to the land of equality."

"I know all that," sighed Mrs. Elton, "but I declare they positively did things better amongst the Indians."

"That is what I am always saying," said Philip Augustus eagerly, "and if you will only let me go back among the Comanche some day, I know it is a much more sensible life than being cooped up in that stupid school and made to spell on a slate, as if I were a child."

"No more of that, my son," said his father sternly, "a decision is not made to be altered. However, it is true enough, Augusta, that the boy is not getting the education he ought to have."

"Do you suppose I am?" asked Selina. "Why, I am fourteen, and the other girls don't have to ask their mothers anything - they go to school or not, as they please, and gad about the town square whenever they've a mind to. Why, Alice Carstairs chooses all her own frocks for herself."

The parents exchanged sober looks. "I will not have you put on Canadian attitudes and become a forward chit such as Alice Carstairs," said Mrs. Elton. "Such independence and impudence in a female child is disgusting."

"But you are female, too, Mama, and you are as independent as any Canadian; more so, for you are the only woman in the country hereabouts who runs a store."

"Your father runs the store," said Mrs. Elton repressively. "And you can see for yourself that I am occupied about the housework."

She rose to clear the plates, and carry them to the wash-tub.

"That is only because Sally left," said Selina pertly.

"Augusta, my dear," said her husband, "we must face facts. It is not the difficulty in obtaining servants - or any of the other inconveniences of Manitoba, that is in question;

surely we experienced far worse on our travels, and we are comfortably enough settled now."

"I should think so!" she said emphatically. "Only think of my store - we are on the way to becoming rich, Philip!"

"Yes, but what does it do to gain the world, and lose oneself? Augusta, the children are not living in a society that can do them any good, or educate them as a lady and a gentleman should be educated; and - I cannot suppose that, occupied as you are - you have observed my situation."

"Your situation?" She was puzzled. "Why, you are a leading man in the neighbourhood, the chief merchant."

"I was never meant for the commercial life - to be in trade, Augusta," he said, bitterly.

"Trade? But you forget, Philip, such distinctions do not matter in Canada. You are a gentleman, though you are in trade; and what does it signify? I tell you, we have full five thousand dollars in capital, and our stock - "

"Listen to me a moment, Augusta. You see I am a minister, without a parish."

"Why, you could preach here if you have a mind," she said crossly.

"No; for here I am tied down with business cares. My own longing to be at home, in England, to pass the latter part of my life by my own fireside, among our own peaceful circle of friends, with their gentle ways, might be taken into account, but it has little importance beside the prospects for our son and daughter. Philip Augustus ought to be preparing for university; Selina ought to be learning accomplishments, and not being spoilt by American manners."

"I don't want to go to university," said Philip Augustus earnestly, "I don't want to be a minister, if you will forgive me, Father; I want to work to help the Indians keep their lands, and not to go back to England at all."

"And you, Selina?" asked Mrs. Elton tartly, "do you mean to marry a trapper or hunter, all in buckskin?"

"If you wish it, Mamma; and I should not mind either if he was as kind to me as dear Pierre and Jean were. But I think that Papa only means that I should learn English ways."

"Yes - I know he does." Mrs. Elton looked at her husband, bald, sad, aging and anxious as he was, and her heart softened. "And so we shall, go home to England, if that is what you think right, Philip."

"Do you mean it, Augusta?" he brightened.

"Indeed I do. We have enough money now, have we not, to be able to live in Highbury again?"

Mr. Elton was so excited, his words almost tripped over each other. "Indeed, indeed we do - and in perfect comfort, what is more. I am still nominal Vicar of the place, and we can afford to keep the curate, and live in the rectory ourselves - perhaps even to make some improvements, with the money we obtain from selling out. Yes, yes. Only one thing, Augusta: I do not know that we should tell people whence it came."

"The money, do you mean?"

"Coming from trade, you know. That would not be considered at all the thing."

"Oh Philip, it will be impossible to explain what our lives have been, to those at Highbury. It is inconceivable that they ever can understand. No; all that sort of thing will take care of itself. We will sell up the store. I believe Flanagan will be very happy to get it, and he has made enough with his blacksmithing and carriage-making, that he should be able to afford to pay a good price."

The rest of the evening was spent in happy plans. From Tawa Town the family would travel by canal and other waterways to Quebec, and visit Pierre and Jean, who were settled there with their families. The winter might be spent in

Quebec, before taking ship for Liverpool in the spring. Philip Augustus, the one of the family least reconciled to the return to England, was at last made to understand that finishing his education would be the wisest course, for if trained as an attorney, he might return to America if he chose and be of real, substantial use to the Indians, as was his dearest wish and plan; and as for Selina, a hint of the beaux she might have, the gowns she might wear, and the balls she might attend, when she came out in two years' time, was enough to fill her head with dreams of the home country which she did not distinctly remember.

CHAPTER TWELVE

*I*n the spring of 1832, the Eltons were settled in Quebec, waiting for the ice to break up, that they might be assured of a safe passage home. Truly it was a comfortable winter; for their trapper friend Pierre now had a comfortable stone house, with his wife Marie-Celestine, and their two babies; Jean was still a bachelor, and spent many of his evenings at his partner's fire, so that the Eltons were with their good friends again, who had helped them and gone through so much with them. They were able to contribute to the household generously; but in fact it was hardly necessary, for both the trappers had done well and were prospering in town, operating their own store.

Quebec was a fine city beyond anything the Eltons had expected. The principal streets were neatly paved with stones, and the lesser ones with planks of pine. There were street-lamps, filled with fish-oil; and the English Cathedral of the Holy Trinity which the Eltons attended, was well heated, with a cast iron stove and warm wood fires. It had also the first peal of bells in the country, and the English-speaking worshipers were as proud of it as the French Canadians were of their own more ancient Basilica, and the Convent of the Ursulines.

The spring brought unusually severe flooding, and the rivers Chaudiere and Etchemin overflowed their bounds so that animals and whole houses were carried away; but the Sergents were safe in the upper part of the town. One evening, they dined comfortably on a couple of ducks Philip Augustus had brought back from a day's shooting in the woods, and the talk was lively.

"Mrs. Elton, I do not know why you must return to your Old Country," said Pierre genially, "Quebec is the best city - we are luxurious, are we not? Such music, such theatres - why, you know that the very best actor in England came and acted in Quebec, not so very long ago."

"Yes, Edmund Kean," Mrs. Elton agreed, "I know he visited Canada; I remember seeing him when I was a young woman in London. Yes, Quebec is quite remarkable in its ideas of society. The dances, and the fashionably late hours, have surprised me, I confess. The people's manners, too, are far better in general than what we have found elsewhere - except among the very newest émigrés, perhaps."

"And as for eating, you will find no finer fare than in Quebec," Pierre nodded.

"Indeed, no - Madame has accomplished wonders with these ducks, and the maple glace," Mrs. Elton acknowledged with a little bow toward her hostess, a shy little French Canadian woman in a lace cap.

"Canada really is a most superior country," agreed Mr. Elton. "There is talk that slavery will be completely outlawed by law in the Lower Canada, next year perhaps - while I really do not believe such a thing will happen in the United States in my lifetime."

"The only thing I can possibly say against Quebec, is the extreme cold of the climate in winter. I don't know how many days there were when the temperature was twenty degrees below zero, and a person's life is quite in danger if one walks out," said Mrs. Elton. Seeing Pierre's face fall, she added quickly, "Of course, if sensible precautions are taken, there need be no discomfort whatever."

"Oh, Mama, surely not, with all the wonderful modern contrivances they have here in winter," protested Philip Augustus. "Why, you can't forget the parties we had on the ice, with our snowshoes; and how comfortable it is in these warm flannel Canadian shirts and moccasins - not a bit of cold can get in."

"And the dog-sled races," put in Selina, "and how we went sliding on Montmorency Falls!"

"You are quiet, Jean," said Mr. Elton keenly observing his friend, "you do not join in singing the praises of your city like the others."

"Yes," said the young man reluctantly, "that is because I have heard some bad news today in the Lower Town. I have been hesitating to break in on our cheerfulness, but I must."

"Tell it quickly, then," said Pierre anxiously. "I have heard there was sickness there - but do not fear, Marie-Celestine, our baby will be well; none of us have been in Lower Town at all this week."

"Many of the houses have been abandoned because of the floods," said Mr. Elton thoughtfully, "and the residents have moved up here. This might tend to spread any illness. Of what sort is it, Jean?"

"The cholera," he said, low.

There was an appalled silence. "Is it very bad?" asked Mrs. Elton apprehensively.

"Bad enough, they say. It started in that dirty boarding-house down in Champlain Street, and good Dr. Fortier is in the thick of it. He expects the epidemic to sweep the city, and talks about a quarantine station."

"We must stay, Pierre?" asked Marie-Celestine timidly.

"I think we will be well enough, *ma chere,* we must lay in a good stock of foodstuffs, and remain as close to home as possible. I do not know that people are advised to leave town, as yet."

"It would only be common sense, as far as possible," said Mr. Elton. "Tomorrow I will go down and see about booking passage in the first ship. After all we have gone through, we must not stay to sicken with the cholera."

"No; certainly not. We residents must take our chance here, but if you can get away as you have been intending, you ought to do so, without delay."

So it was decided; and the following evening Mr. Elton, his face well wrapped up against the encroaching plague, reported to his anxious family.

"It is as bad as possible down there," he said, "a dozen more cases; but I have booked passage on the *Hesperia*, to go the twentieth of June. Pray God we will escape. The people are panicked and ships are not being permitted to land - we will have to journey around to Grosse Isle for our boarding."

It was not a gay leave-taking. In fear and solemnity did the Eltons pack their boxes, and convey them down to the ship, anxiously trying to have the least contact possible with any of the people in the streets. The parting with their French Canadian friends was sad and sore, but all parties were so well aware of its necessity that lamentations were almost perfunctory. And at last, the Eltons were aboard ship, enjoying a crossing which, in the event, proved blessedly serene, and not marked with illness or any other danger.

Four weeks from that time, they were at Liverpool, almost bewildered by hearing English voices once again, and seeing English buildings and people all around them. A rapid progress by coach, and before the beautiful and golden month of July had closed, they were once again at home, in Highbury.

CHAPTER THIRTEEN

*I*t passes belief," said Mrs. Knightley to Mrs. Weston, "to conceive that Mrs. Elton will soon be here once more."

They were seated with their husbands at a little table set out in the garden at Donwell, enjoying the fragrance of the roses, now at their height, and admiring the delicate fritillaries and lavender.

"It does, indeed. How we shall enjoy hearing about the Eltons' American adventures. Highbury will never have heard anything like them before, and every conversation is sure to be about the Eltons, for many a day."

In spite of the lovely afternoon and the beauties of her garden, Emma could not look pleased, she so disliked the prospect of seeing Mrs. Elton again. "I hope not," she said sourly, "I do not want to talk about anything to do with Mrs. Elton on a constant or even a semi-constant basis."

"My dear Emma - only think. She may have improved. After such ordeals as she has gone through, one can hardly suspect that she would not have changed greatly."

"The ordeals have been terrible indeed," put in Mr. Knightley, soberly, "to judge by the letter friend Elton has sent me. Their encounters with the Indians alone - I cannot make known all that he said, it is too frightful, but it should be enough to make us very thankful that their lives were spared."

"Do you really mean that Mrs. Elton and her children lived among the Indians for years?" Emma put in incredulously.

"That is what the letter says."

"Good God! How, then, can you talk of Mrs. Elton improving, Mrs. Weston? Her manners were unpleasing before, but now that she has lived among savages she must be infinitely worse."

"That remains to be seen, Emma, but I think the Eltons will have the best right of telling us of their experiences themselves, and we must not judge them prematurely."

"Oh! certainly not," she said, disagreeably.

A round, bustling figure could be seen approaching from the direction of the Martins' farm, and Mrs. Martin appeared, carrying a basket, her face red and hot from her walk.

"Why, Harriet! You have had a warm walk," said Emma kindly. "Will not you sit down and take some of this cool ginger drink? And some lemon biscuits."

"Oh - yes - thank you, Mrs. Knightley; and I have brought you some new peas from our garden, they are specially good. Robert said so himself. Have you heard the news?"

Emma sighed. "I daresay it is about the Eltons, as everything now seems to be. We have heard they are to be in Highbury any day now."

"Mr. Cole had a letter. Did not Mr. Knightley? Oh - I thought he should. Well," continued Harriet, "Mr. Cole's letter said - I am not sure, exactly - but I believe it told about how Mr. Elton was scalped by the Indians! Only think how horrible! And so we are to be warned that his appearance is very much altered, and not be too much shocked."

"Scalped!" every one exclaimed at once. Mr. Knightley shook his head and said, low, to Mrs. Weston, "That was the news I wished to conceal."

"What else did Mr. Cole say?" asked Emma, unable to help her curiosity.

"Oh! Ever so much more. La! I cannot recollect it all. That Mrs. Elton lived with the Indians, and wore buckskin and moccasins like a savage; and washed with ashes and ate bear and snake and all sorts of horrid things. And Philip Augustus was made an honorary Indian. I wonder if he scalped anyone himself? I remember that he really was a very untamed little boy. Oh, and Mrs. Elton ran a shop - not when she was with the Indians, I don't think - but it is true she really was a shopkeeper and helped behind the counter herself. Yes, and they ran away from a dreadful cholera epidemic, and they saw slaves in the Southern states, real slaves, only imagine how horrid."

"If even one quarter of that remarkable narrative is true," said Emma dryly, "you are perfectly right, Mrs. Weston, Highbury will never stop talking about it.

"Do you think Highbury will receive Mrs. Elton in society?" Harriet asked eagerly. "I mean - a woman who has waited in a shop - it is not very nice, after all."

"There can be no question of that," said Mr. Knightley firmly. "The churchwardens have agreed, without a demur, that Mr. Elton is to have his living back; that has all been decided. Mrs. Elton will be our vicar's wife, as before, and of course they shall be accepted by us all, the more because of the sad trials they have endured."

"We must feel sympathy for Mrs. Elton, Emma," said Mrs. Weston gently, "she lost a child to the Indians, did not she."

Emma remained unpersuaded. She could have wished that the Eltons had stayed in America forever, and she dreaded the changes that would surely come to Highbury from their re-introduction.

Yet Mrs. Weston's prediction seemed the most likely to come true. The Eltons returned, and were comfortably settled once more at the vicarage, as nearly as possible as if they had never been away. Their kind neighbours allowed only a short time to elapse, for the purpose of rest and refreshment, before dinner invitations from Donwell, Hartfield, Randalls and all of Highbury began to shower down upon them.

Mrs. Elton might almost boast again, as she did upon her original arrival in Highbury, of never having a disengaged day; and at the first dinner at Donwell, she did indeed appear a changed being, not only in her looks, but because there was so much for her to hear of changes in Highbury, that she submitted to listen quietly, and to refrain from any shocking recitals of her American adventures. Indeed, Mrs. Weston's description of Mr. Frank Churchill's marriage to a Yorkshire heiress, which made him richer than ever, took up some little time, encompassing as it did the couple's plans to live in London, and the social prospects of Miss Jane Churchill, which would be ample. While this was going on, Mr. Elton made free in his discourse on American conditions to the other gentlemen; but to Emma, the sight of Mrs. Elton, listening calmly and saying little, was perhaps the greatest novelty of all.

Emma had concealed her first shock at the Eltons' appearance, but she knew she was not the only one to feel it. They had been away some seven years, it was true, but decades seemed to have passed over Mr. Elton's bald and scarred pate. Weathered and aged as he looked, however, his expression was peaceful, one of content at being again home; and the sermon he preached on the first Sunday after his return, was a simple and heartfelt one of thanksgiving.

Mrs. Elton looked less old and ill than her husband, but she too was an altered creature. Thin, sun-browned and coarsened, one might expect her to be; but as well, the simple cotton gown she had hastily purchased ready-made at Liverpool, with more thought to utility than fashion, formed a striking contrast with her elegant lace gowns of the past. Her hands were roughened, bespeaking the work she had done herself, and her movements were rough too, not as concealed and graceful as the other women's; she seated herself, and walked, and gestured, like someone who had come from a free and easy land where no thought was ever given to such matters as deportment. Her eyes had a keenness and activity that had been altogether lacking in the old days; but one thing was unchanged, and that was her assurance.

Mrs. Elton had ever been sure of herself, to the point of being insufferable in Emma's eyes; but even Emma had to admit that the woman's new confidence was of a different order, or so she thought it would prove. She had an air of being capable of anything, up to anything, as Emma supposed she must be, in sober truth, after such experiences; even when she was only seated quietly, her eyes resting proudly on her children, she had a masterful look, which Emma did not like at all.

Emma followed Mrs. Elton's gaze, toward her children, and her thoughts turned to wondering what these Americanised young people would mean to Highbury. For Philip Augustus was a handsome, active young man, who drew the eyes of all the young girls, sheltered as they were, never having seen his like before. Mrs. Weston's Anna and Emily, Isabella's youngest daughters Susan and Rose, all displayed identical expressions of rapt enchantment.

"Will Philip Augustus be going to university?" was an early question of Mr. Knightley's, and the answer appeared to be that he would go to a tutor for a year, and then to Oxford. Emma's eyes turned to fifteen-year-old Selena, a pretty girl with forward American manners in which no vestige of shyness showed itself; she was indeed Mrs. Elton's daughter, Emma thought to herself wryly, watching the girl. Selina almost bounced with expectation when Mr. Weston spoke of getting up a dance.

"You will have to show us the American dances," Mrs. Weston told her kindly.

"Oh! but I hope someone will show me the English ones too," she brightly made answer, without hesitation. "I love to dance, and did so among the Indians and also in Tawa Town and Quebec; but there we mostly jumped about, and I am sure the English dances must be more refined. Will you teach me to dance, Mr. Knightley?" she addressed the Knightleys' oldest son, Henry, who stood by her side and gazed down at the rosy-cheeked, curly-haired girl admiringly, for all that he was a Cambridge man, six or seven years older than she.

"A gentleman does not teach a young lady to dance, in England," Emma interposed austerely, "but I daresay you will learn fast enough."

"Why, Emma, my girls can give her a bit of instruction," said Mrs. Weston good-naturedly.

"Certainly; let us go into the ball-room now, if you like it; should you, Miss Elton?" said tall, stately Anna, while her younger sister Emily nodded eagerly.

"I should like nothing better; but we need music, do we not?"

"I will play," said Anna, "and Emily can show you the figures. Come, then," and the girls ran away laughing.

Mr. Elton looked fondly at his wife. "Never mind but Selina will do well wherever she is," he assured her. Mrs. Elton only smiled. "No, I am not worried about Selina," she said.

"Oh; no, she will do very well indeed - once something is done about that accent," Mrs. Knightley assured her condescendingly.

Mrs. Elton was not to be drawn. "We are meaning to make her a parlour-boarder at Miss Goddard's school for a year or two; that will smooth down some of the American-ness," she said calmly. "Do not you think that will be a good plan?"

"Oh! but you have not heard," said Mrs. Martin, "that Miss Goddard is no more. No, she was took with a violent pain in her head three years ago this Michaelmas, and was gone in a fortnight, poor soul. Mr. Perry did all that he could but he thinks it was water upon the brain. Ah! We are growing sadly old and ill, and that is what we all must come to, in the end," she shook her head. "Mrs. Bates is dead you know - and Miss Bates is quite an invalid; she has had a paralytic stroke poor soul, and cannot talk."

"I am sorry indeed to hear that," said Mrs. Elton, concerned. "Poor good Miss Bates; I will visit her tomorrow, if I may. And Miss Goddard is a sad loss. However, the school carries on, I comprehend?"

"Oh, yes, the school is still there, to be sure; the under-teacher, Miss Bickerton, who used to be at school with me in the old days, has took it over, and runs it quite as well, and will be very glad to take Miss Elton, I make no doubt. She will be a very bright pupil, if only, well I am not quite sure; her manners - Miss Bickerton may make some difficulties about them, for that American speech is not quite refined, you know. But I have no fear but that it will not be corrected in time, so that she may be fit to come out one day and make her appearance in society."

"I do not know about coming out, it is rather early to think about such things. Our Selina is but fifteen, and has English life to learn all over again. There is no hurry."

"But a girl of fifteen, with everything to learn! My dear Mrs. Elton, what an infinity there is to accomplish before she is fit for London!" Harriet lifted her hands.

"I doubt that Mr. Elton will consider a season in London as appropriate for a clergyman's daughter," said Mrs. Elton, collectedly, "and we mean not to go to any extraordinary expenses, but to be prudent. We shall be very glad to keep the child at home for some time to come."

"And she will have no lack of beaux in Highbury, certainly," admitted Emma, rather reluctantly, "for if nothing else she is a very pretty girl, and I can already see that my boys admire... Why! Where are Henry and John?"

"I believe they followed the girls into the ball-room," said Mrs. Weston.

"Heavens! Mr. Knightley, you had better go after them. No ball was intended tonight, and there are no chaperones. Very improper behaviour; I am sure I cannot answer for the consequences."

Mr. Knightley, followed by his wife, strode to the ballroom, and there beheld all the young men of the party in a circle around Selina, who was performing a wild dance of a style never seen in Highbury before, whirling hand in hand with young Henry Knightley, who tried awkwardly to follow while he gazed on her with an air of most unmistakable admiration.

"There - that is how the Comanches celebrate a feast," she laughed, collapsing into a seated position on the floor, her skirts around her, indifferent to the display of her pretty ankles. "Though to be sure we never got such good victuals among them as we have had here tonight. Now, Johnny Knightley, you may whirl me next - is it not great fun!"

"Well, I should say," exclaimed the youth, before his father stepped forward and put an end to the revels.

The Knightleys returned to the drawing-room, Mr. Knightley looking amused, his lady extremely annoyed. "We found Miss Elton teaching the boys Indian dances," was all

Emma attempted to say, and Mrs. Elton gestured her wayward daughter to her side, with a little shake of her head.

Only Philip Augustus laughed. "My sister has so much spirit; she loves to laugh and dance, and I do believe it was this quality, her natural buoyancy, that carried her through all our hardships."

"I am sure it was," said Mrs. Weston gently, "but we must teach her that Indian ways do not always serve in England. You will remember this another time, I am sure, Miss Elton, won't you?"

"I'll try, Mrs. Weston," returned Selina, her eyes sparkling.

"Your hardships - your travails - " Emma addressed Mrs. Elton, hoping to give the conversation a less frivolous tone. "They have been something dreadful, we are given to understand."

"Oh, there were some bad times, I do not deny it," said Mrs. Elton easily, "when we were first captured, that was the worst. But there was much to enjoy. You cannot conceive what a wonderful country America is - America and the Canadas. Such beauty, such freedom, such glorious wilderness!"

"I prefer the calm beauty of Sussex," said Emma coldly.

"Ah, that is because you have never seen how the frosts paint the American woods with brilliant colours," cried Mrs. Elton. "And the people, and their manners - why, only think of a country where all are equal, and there is no cringing subservience of the lower orders, no dictatorial arrogance of the higher. Everyone is considered the same, and servants dine at table with their masters."

"Do they, really?" asked Mrs. Knightley, looking at the speaker with pity.

Philip Augustus laughed. "Why, Mama, you are not being quite sincere. You know it took you some time yourself to get used to that custom!"

"That is true; but now that I have learned the true meaning of democracy, it is difficult to go back to the old-fashioned ways. And you know you agree with me my dear; you, who are always talking of returning to the Comanche."

"So I shall, one day, when I am an attorney, and in a position to do some good," her son said quietly.

"Are you to be an attorney?" Mr. John Knightley spoke up for the first time that day, his eyes lighting up with interest.

"Yes, sir. It is my intention to learn all I can about treaty law."

"A very interesting study. You shall be welcome to read law with me, my boy. None of my sons have chosen it for their profession, which I regret, but I should like to have an interest in the education of a young man such as yourself."

"I only hope you will not take one of our girls back into the wilderness with you," murmured his wife. "It is so very dangerous. It is what I should never like for Bella. What would my dear father have said!"

"Since he objected to every little thing that smacked of venturesomeness, my dear Isabella, even to a window being left open, it is fairly certain that Mr. Woodhouse would have been appalled at the mere thought of any of his descendants going off to the wilderness," said Mr. John Knightley dryly, "but we may flatter ourselves that it may not happen."

Philip Augustus thanked Mr. John Knightley for his kindness, and made no mention of any wish to take a wife back to America with him, although both Anna and Emily did their best to show him with their eyes that they would not at all mind being chosen for a life among savages, if they might be accompanied by some one who had such snapping black eyes, and such a fine tall person, as young Mr. Elton. In truth, the young man had inherited his father's early handsomeness, along with something resembling his mother's enterprising spirit, cast in a new form.

Here we must leave Highbury; but be it known that Mrs. Elton resumed her old place in the town and, in time, found her own level, which was not essentially different from that of former years; and that even though she had become a wiser and more prudent woman from her American experiences, Mrs. Knightley never learned to like her. This proved to be an unfortunate circumstance, as within the course of a few years they were united by family ties, of bond and blood, for the lively, bright-eyed Selina, after leading all the young gentlemen a merry dance as belle of the neighbourhood, married Mrs. Knightley's eldest son George, and for ever afterward she appeared to the older Mrs. Knightley in the guise of that most odious of portents, the future mistress of Donwell.

Philip Augustus did not take a bride from the Highbury neighbourhood, but he did fulfil his early dreams of emigrating to America, where he served in the Bureau of Indian Affairs before rising to Senator of his chosen state, and finished as a distinguished Cabinet member under Abraham Lincoln. In his time, he knew Dickens, Twain, Carlyle and Alexander Graham Bell; and he frequently journeyed to London where he delivered speeches before Parliament on behalf of his adopted country. He was altogether so distinguished a man as to quite rejoice the heart of his proud mother and father, removed from the stream of great world events as they were in Highbury, and content to bask from afar in the accomplishments of Philip Augustus Elton. They lived to see him a famed Civil War orator in the Union cause; and themselves great-grandparents with descendants on both sides of the ocean. But Mrs. Knightley was never tired of remarking, in her outspoken old age, that America had done the Eltons' manners no good at all.

ALSO BY **DIANA BIRCHALL**
AND
PUBLISHED BY
EGERTON HOUSE

MRS. DARCY'S DILEMMA
ISBN: 090501600X

Five and twenty years after her marriage, Elizabeth is as much as ever the delight of Mr. Darcy's mind and the beloved of his heart. But in the affairs of her children, visits from her nieces, and a theatrical scandal, Mrs. Darcy finds much to occupy herself in the new Victorian age that is opening upon Pemberley...

PRAISE FOR DIANA BIRCHALL'S
PRIDE AND PREJUDICE SEQUEL

"*Mrs. Darcy's Dilemma* - the very title makes you want to read it right away!...Fascinating, and such **wonderful** use of language." - *Joan Austen-Leigh*

"Birchall's **witty**, elegant visit to the middle-aged Darcys is a delight."- *Professor Janet Todd* University of Glasgow

"A refreshing and entertaining look at the Darcys some years after *Pride and Prejudice* from a most **accomplished** author." - *Jenny Scott*, author of *After Jane*

Available online at Amazon

Other Austen Sequels published by Egerton House

THE DARCYS – SCENES FROM MARRIED LIFE
After Jane Austen's Pride and Prejudice
by Phyllis Furley
ISBN: 0954627571
AVAILABLE FROM AMAZON NOW

The Darcys' first two years of marriage come close to fulfilling Elizabeth's lighthearted claim that they will be "The happiest married couple in the world."
But not without some painful trials.

At Pemberley Elizabeth is somewhat oppressed by the weight of centuries of tradition. Furthermore, she is scrutinised by senior members of Darcy's family. Those amiable family members, Georgiana and Colonel Fitzwilliam, are ready for marriage. (To each other?)

The greatest challenge is unforeseen. A shadow from Darcy's past looks to darken the future.

FITZWILLIAM DARCY'S MEMOIRS
An insight into Jane Austen's hero
by Juliette Shapiro
ISBN: 0954627504
RELEASE DATE - JULY 2004

1853. The mistress of Pemberley, is dead. Mr Darcy, at sixty-eight, who is very properly impressed by the fact that he will never look upon her fine eyes again, begins a journal. In it he records the private details of his loss and then, as a means to honour Elizabeth's memory, sets about the task of writing about their life together.

Fitzwilliam Darcy's Memoirs offers hitherto unknown insights into the mind, the heart, and the home of a man more commonly thought of as reserved.

DONWELL ABBEY
A Victorian Sequel to Jane Austen's Emma
by Katharine Moore
ISBN: 1905016026
RELEASE DATE - JULY 2004

Emma Knightley, though now a grandmother, retains the most attractive characteristics of her youth - humour, vigour and kindness are evident in her dealings with the younger generation and combine with a trace of her former tendency to manage other people's lives. And a touch of management is certainly needed to assist the love affairs and destinies of her own grandchildren and the descendants of old acquaintances such as the Elliots, the Tilneys, the Martins and the unspeakable Eltons.

Egerton House Publishing
E-Mail: books@egertonhousepublishing.co.uk

Printed in the United States
114846LV00004B/53/A